WHAT PEOPLE ARE SAYING ABOUT

TO FEAR, WITH LOVE

Helen's gripping book is a story of addiction in all its forms and will strike a chord with anyone who has found themselves trapped in a damaging relationship.
**Monica Long**, Development Producer, Comedy Entertainment, Hat Trick Productions

What a page turner. Gripped me from beginning to end. Helen Jane Rose is extremely talented and I can't wait for her next book. Her characters are so easily identifiable. I couldn't put the book down! Brilliant.
**Hannah Peddar**, Production Manager, Have I Got News For You

A captivating story of awakening the power within, breaking the chains of control and living the ultimate experience of love. Wonderfully descriptive and inspirational, Helen Jane Rose has produced an enlightened book with a message for us all.
**Louise Segui**, Holistic Physiotherapist, Reiki Master-Teacher of 2Evolve Wellbeing Centre & Hale Clinic

If ever there was a love story that needed to be told, this is quite simply it. The mere fact I was vigorously turning pages into the night and way past 3.00am firmly says it all. I was hooked. As an author, Helen Jane Rose writes with such authenticity she represents 'the voice' of many women in her main character's fearful predicament. *To Fear, With Love* hits all the pressure points when it comes to dealing with terror in a so-called 'loving' relationship. With frightening overtones masking visual scenes of grandeur and luxurious opulence, one firmly believes Alice has really paid the price, quite literally. However, it's the buckets of justice against all odds and the perfect ending that makes it a must read for those in search of self-discovery, spiritual healing and courage to find their way out.

As cliché as it sounds, the power of love, in all its capacities, really can conquer all in more ways than we give it credit for. I loved the book and so many others will too. Helen Jane Rose is most definitely the female author to watch out for this year.

**Kate Marshall**, Freelance Writer, Editor and Producer

# To Fear,
# With Love

# To Fear, With Love

Helen Jane Rose

ROUNDFIRE
BOOKS

Winchester, UK
Washington, USA

First published by Roundfire Books, 2014
Roundfire Books is an imprint of John Hunt Publishing Ltd., Laurel House, Station Approach,
Alresford, Hants, SO24 9JH, UK
office1@jhpbooks.net
www.johnhuntpublishing.com
www.roundfire-books.com

For distributor details and how to order please visit the 'Ordering' section on our website.

Text copyright: Helen Jane Rose 2013

ISBN: 978 1 78279 581 0

A CIP catalogue record for this book is available from the British Library.

Design: Stuart Davies

Printed in the USA by Edwards Brothers Malloy

We operate a distinctive and ethical publishing philosophy in all
areas of our business, from our global network of authors to
production and worldwide distribution.

In dedication to Alice Bailey
For holding the vision of a unified world and encouraging others to do the same, through inner reflection and outward action, to bring about solutions to humanity's biggest problems. Her ageless wisdom is very much alive today through the Lucis Trust which she founded in 1922 with husband Foster Bailey. The trust is on the Roster of the United Nations Economic and Social Council. The fictional character in To Fear, With Love is not in any way based on the life and work of Alice A. Bailey.

In tribute to Princess Diana
In remembrance of her living kindness and compassion and her legacy that united the hearts of nations.

"There are two basic motivating forces: fear and love. When we are afraid, we pull back from life. When we are in love, we open to all that life has to offer."

John Lennon

"I believe that every single event in life happens as an opportunity to choose love over fear."
Oprah Winfrey

# PART ONE

## The Prelude

# I

# The Interview (a journalist's perspective)

I wanted to make her feel as comfortable as possible. She looked so regal sitting there poised on the edge of the sofa. My long-held ambition to interview Alice Bailey was finally coming true – she was sat opposite me ready to tell the truth about her past and share some of her most intimate thoughts.

As she smiled, her whole face lit up and I wondered if it was possible for someone to look and be as graceful as this beautiful woman. I still wasn't sure where to start. Night after night I had thought about what to ask her. I needed to cover her life and particularly her earlier years – simple enough yet complex considering how much she had achieved.

I decided to work backwards; if for no other reason than I knew so much about her later years, but her past I'd only ever read snippets about. I don't know why I was worrying so much, after all she had agreed to the project and knew she needed to be open about some of the traumatic times in her life. I felt so excited to be interviewing her and still couldn't believe that Alice Bailey was sitting in front of me. I'd met many a celebrity through my job and quite honestly had never been star struck, but this was different. This was someone who had been made famous for wanting to make a difference to people's lives and the respect I held for her was far greater than any other famous person I had ever met before. She was always so passionate and full of life and I found her enthusiasm infectious. She had been such an inspiration to me and I knew there were millions of others who felt the same way. You only had to look at the television ratings to realize that whenever she was interviewed she commanded a huge audience. People wanted to hear honesty and that's what they got with Alice Bailey. There was no PR spin, she never worried about what she should or shouldn't say, she just told the truth – and yes sometimes it was brutal but that made the viewing all the more interesting.

It was a strange feeling knowing that we were going to spend the next four days together, and I wondered how much time she would need away from my voice recorder. As I set everything up I watched her staring out of the window, sipping delicately on her tea. She was a strange mix of someone extremely gentle yet stronger than anyone else I had ever met before. It was an inner strength rather than an outward show of muscle – an inner resolve that would stop at nothing to achieve her goals. She cared little about what people thought of her, and I couldn't help thinking that was the very reason that had drawn people to her in the first place.

"I don't want to waste any of your time, Alice, are you ready to start?" I asked bringing her attention back into the room.

I'd been stung too many times by faulty equipment to rely on just one portable recorder. I checked my back-up was in working order and pressed play – it was too good an opportunity to miss even a word.

"Were you told that I only agreed to do this if you were the one interviewing me? I don't mind who does the final editing but I do care who I spend four days with. I've always admired your work," she said looking directly at me.

I was taken aback. I had no idea that she had specifically requested that I do the interviewing. I knew we were breaking new ground by a newspaper publishing an autobiography, but assumed I had been given the job based on my fascination with her. Not for one minute did I suspect she had actually asked for me.

"No one told me that you'd specifically asked for me. I'm really flattered. I don't understand why they didn't tell me."

"I'm sure I ruffled a few feathers and know who they had planned for me. I found an hour in his company difficult enough,

4

let alone four days. I'm afraid I have a bad reaction to big egos. He's the epitome of a Mr. Know-It-All and I hate the way he shouts at everyone across the office. It's as if he believes his job title gives him the right to treat everyone with contempt. Do you know who I'm talking about?"

"You're talking about the deputy editor, aren't you?" I said hesitantly hoping she wasn't talking about someone else.

"Don't you think he's like a little man that needs to feel big by putting everyone else down all the time? There's a lady too that works alongside him who actually seems more of a vulture than he is?"

"I know exactly who you mean – Sarah Danes. Most of us are frightened of her. I've always just accepted that their attitude's what's needed to get the paper out," I said flippantly, wanting to move the conversation on.

"So you believe that ruling with an iron fist is the way to motivate people and get the best out of them?" she said sounding slightly irritated.

"To be honest I've never really thought about it. Since the day I started in this industry I've always come up against bosses who manage like tyrants. I've just come to accept it."

"Do you enjoy your job?"

"When I'm out of the office interviewing people I love it. I get stressed when I've spent too much time at my desk. Part of me would have walked a long time ago but it was always my dream to work on a national – I'd feel like a failure if I left now. I guess it just goes with the job?"

She seemed to have a knack of getting you to open up without even realizing you'd done it. Before I had thought about what I was saying I had answered her, and felt unprofessional as a result – yet I trusted that she would keep the information to herself.

"You write with passion, is that your motivating factor for being a journalist?"

"I suppose so. To be honest I just see it as a job I'm good at."

"You must be aware of some of the changes that have come about because of your features?"

"It does make me feel good, but also despondent. Really I'm making no difference at all."

"That's not true. Think of how many people you've helped just through what you've written so far."

"If you put it like that then I guess it's true. But I never really thought about journalism as being able to help people?" I said, feeling a bit stupid.

"Why not?" she said seeming surprised.

"Because we're all too obsessed with getting a good story and then getting it to print as quickly as possible. It's so cutthroat and I can only write about what's going to sell. No one's really interested in feel good stories – they want the gory details of the latest murder or info about the most recent round of job casualties. "

"Do they?" she said raising her eyebrows as she spoke.

"I sense sarcasm in your voice," I said smiling at her.

"We're at a point where every page in every paper talks of doom and gloom. Where's the balance? Is it all that bad, is there really nothing to be excited about or look forward to? Are we really a nation that's depressed? Where are the voices trying to raise that negativity, trying to show the positive aspects of life? Newspapers are so quick to fire the blame at other people but where's their responsibility in all of this? If I'd just lost my job would I really want to be reminded of how bad life was, or would I want to be uplifted and given a glimmer of hope?"

"You know the nickname that flies around the office about you?" I asked tentatively, hoping I didn't sound rude.

"Little Miss-Fix-It?" she said the second after I'd finished speaking.

"I thought that was just an in-house tag that everyone wished they could use about you, but can't." I was surprised that she knew.

"I know that I'm treated with contempt by many influential people, but I couldn't care less. I can't live without meaning in my life, it's up to them how they view what I do."

"I admire the fact that they don't dare print anything negative about you," I said, hoping she would explain why.

"And why do you think that is?"

"It's one that's baffled me. We're so quick to attack anyone that tries to do something good, but with you it's different."

"That's because your publisher and a few others within the paper are good friends of mine. They're loyal to me and genuinely like what we're doing. There are many people out there who want to see change and are covertly backing what we do – even people in the government who publicly argue against us, privately feed us information. Sorry, I've sidetracked us. Where do you want me to start?"

"So much has gone on for you of late. I obviously read about Sam committing suicide, is that something you'd be happy to talk about?"

"I don't mind talking about it but I don't want it to be the focus of the book. What he did was atrocious and he deserved to be put in prison. The fact that he committed suicide was a way out from facing up to what he had done. His temper could get so out of control that I used to be frightened of how far he'd go to vent his anger on me. Can you imagine living like that? Scared that the person you're married to could be the very same person that could end up killing you? I lived silently in fear of him for many years before I got the courage to leave."

"I feel uncomfortable delving too much into your private life. Perhaps it's best for a while that you just talk and I record what you say, if you're happy to do it that way, Alice?"

"I was given strict instructions to tell all about my journey to supposed stardom and am happy to do so. Isn't it funny how we're a nation that's obsessed with celebrities, but we're never really told about their inevitable struggles on the path to their success? It's as if 'poof' in a split second they became a pop star or an actor – fame that was just handed to them on a silver plate. People forget that life can be tough for everyone, especially now, and I really want to get that across. We live in a world where most people only dream of what they could become and that's the problem. Everything takes effort and work; there isn't a single person that isn't thrown challenges from life. I wish I knew more about people's journeys to success. Isn't a person made inter-esting by their story, by the path they've trodden – by what's been thrown at them and what they've overcome? Isn't that what it's really about?"

This woman had a depth to her that I knew I'd find hard to follow. She seemed to have a view of the world that was a far cry from most people's perceptions, and a strength of character that was so independent that you didn't dare question her. There was an authority in her voice that made you want to understand everything that she said, but I knew this wasn't what they wanted for the book. Their aim was to show that Little-Miss-Fix-It had had it rough.

I felt under pressure to focus our conversation or the result of our four days together would end in me out of a job. I could already imagine my editor reading what we had covered so far and throwing the transcript back at me. I had to get to the nitty-gritty so we could logically build a picture of her life.

She was staring at a painting on the wall and looked as if she was in deep thought about it. It was a picture of a naked couple kissing standing facing each other, with the man's hands on the woman's breasts. I hadn't noticed it before and thought it was a bit blatant, but I shouldn't have been surprised because the place was quirky in every sense. It was her choice of venue for our four days together and I could see why. It had a relaxed, cozy atmos-phere, but was very chic at the same time. Incense sticks burned throughout the lobby and huge cushions replaced chairs, whilst the sofas in the bar looked more like beds.

"I love that picture," she said, as she stood up to get a closer look. "I must ask Madeline where she bought it. It's a sensual picture isn't it? Do you enjoy sex?"

I could feel my cheeks going red and my body temperature rise. It wasn't often that I felt shy or embarrassed but she had completely shocked me. I knew we'd get onto the subject at some point knowing how openly she talked about her sex life, but I hadn't expected her to focus on me. I was used to asking the awkward questions and didn't really know how to answer her.

"I suppose so," I said, trying to say as little as possible. "To be honest I'm too tired most of the time. I guess that's just what happens when you're in a long-term relationship?"

"It's a shame isn't it? The one thing that relieves stress and brings people closer together is pushed aside whilst we focus on the things that cause us unhappiness and make us feel apprehensive."

"I think it's more to do with being exhausted than anything else," I replied, trying to justify what I had said.

"But aren't people feeling exhausted because they've forgotten how to have fun?"

"Please don't think I'm being rude but most people don't have time to think about having fun. Whichever way you look at it life's a nightmare for most people at the moment, especially from a financial point of view."

"I understand what you're saying but sex is magical and ignites passion, and what's more it's free!" She laughed as she spoke and her whole face smiled.

"I remember when I loved having sex," I said opening up a bit more.

"I remember when I hated having sex and now I love it. Sorry I've sidetracked the conversation. Do you want to ask me some questions?"

"Do you mind if we talk about Sam?"

"No, fire away."

"Was it true that Sam had a drug problem? Was he an addict when you first got together?"

"Sam lived life to the extreme. I wouldn't say he was an addict but he did get more dependent when we moved to St Kitts. If truth be told it was me who was the addict, not him. I used it as an escape but it got completely out of hand and I couldn't break its hold over me. That's how I came to view it. I knew I was strong deep down but I felt weak every time I had an urge to boost my mood, which quickly became every day. The goody two-shoes image that's been created about me isn't quite true. In a way I'm now thankful for the experience because it drove me to find meaning in my life. When I finally made the decision to get help I was an emotional wreck, and it was really tough at the beginning. I felt patronized and a failure for not being able to control what I was doing – but people who haven't been in that position can't understand it. It's too easy to brand someone as an addict and look down on them, but there's always a reason why you end up there. No one goes out of their way to become dependent on something they can't control. I've still got a habit that I don't want to quit – would you mind if I go outside for a cigarette soon?"

"You've kept that quiet," I said, surprised that she smoked.

"Don't you see what's happened in the press? It's as if editors across the country have made a pact to portray me as butter-wouldn't-melt – but it's not true. I have my vices and would be the first to admit I enjoy a cigarette. I'm not proud that I smoke but between you and me I like it, and until I don't I know I won't be able to give up. If they printed a picture of me smoking it would ruin the image they've created. I'd prefer it if they did."

"Surely if you want to create a different image of yourself you have the power to plant a story or picture in the press?" I said slightly indignantly but not wanting to offend her.

"You know the game better than most – of course it's possible but in all honesty I play the press just like they play me. I need them to help publicize what we're doing so I'm careful not to smoke openly, but it's becoming more difficult."

"I'm so sorry to cut you off but can we talk about your time living in St Kitts?"

"Yes, of course we can. I know they want sensation with this book but that's not really why I agreed to do it. I've been made into a celebrity and feel I have a responsibility to show people honestly that my rise to fame was anything but easy. I also really want them to realize that anyone in the limelight is a normal person with the same hang-ups, emotions and hurdles as everyone else. My life was really tough and it's only been recently that things have changed for me. It was a struggle for so long and I even came close to giving up on life completely at one point."

"Would you be comfortable to talk about that?"

"Yes. I was at a point when my self-esteem was very low. I believed all the brutal things that Sam said about me and had allowed the relationship to deteriorate so badly that if he wasn't mentally torturing me he was physically attacking me. I felt like a caged bird whose escape was impossible, and all the while I was trying to pretend to the outside world that everything was great. At that point I seriously considered suicide. I was in a catch-22 situation – if I was weak around him he took more advantage of me but if I became strong and stood up to him he became more aggressive. So I decided that being passive was the easiest option, but it ate away at me until the night when I decided that there was only one way out. I'd thought about it many times before, but it was something I only daydreamed about, believing it to be the ultimate escape. I didn't actually attempt to commit suicide but the thought of trying to plan it woke me up to the reality that I had found myself in. After that I vowed to do whatever it took to get away from Sam. It all happened in a roundabout way, through a friend at the time. He helped me to find the strength to leave Sam and deal with the consequences."

# II

# The Book Launch (Alice Bailey's perspective) One year on...

I was stunned by how many people were in the room. The lights blinded my full vision, but as I looked around I couldn't believe how many people had made the effort to turn up. It was a gossip journalist's dream but no one had come to talk about themselves – or each other. They had come to support my book knowing how much their faces would help.

It was a strange launch that I wanted to get over and done with as soon as possible – the idea being that I read the first chapter of the book to publicize the audio version that was going on sale at exactly the same time, to reach as wide an audience as possible from the outset. I wanted to be mingling but I had a job to do and the publishers wanted more than their money's worth when it came to promoting my autobiography. I had an agenda too and knew I needed to get maximum publicity out of the evening.

"Oh wow, what a coup. Guess who's over there?" Stephanie my publicist said trying to whisper in my ear.

"Are you talking about James?" I asked trying to follow her stare.

"Perhaps he's James to you, darling – to me he will only ever be the ex-president of the United States. This is fantastic, what the hell is he doing here? Surely he doesn't need the publicity?"

"He's a good friend of mine, Stephanie. He's helped us so much. I'm glad he could come, but I wasn't expecting him to show up, which is why I didn't say anything to you. They're not all motivated by fame and money you know. Most of the people you're looking at want to make some kind of difference. They've made their money, endured the fame and now want to give something back to make their lives feel worthwhile." She looked at me as if I was speaking in another language but I didn't need her to understand. She had done her job, and everyone standing in front of us – to all their credit – had made the effort to be at my launch.

Of course the event wasn't without the usual media whores, and I laughed as I saw Chloe Jones working the crowd. She was brilliant at her job. She had the gift of getting anyone to open up to her and had caused a lot of damage as a result. But her infamous thirty-second questioning was beginning to make her job harder, as I watched people deliberately avoiding her. I'm not sure if it was her amazing looks or reputation that had gained her the quotes that most journalists would kill for – but time was definitely running out for her on the celebrity circuit. She had burned too many bridges and I guessed she would soon be reinventing herself. She was so talented yet her arrogance meant she had little respect for anyone, and now it was working against her.

"How the hell did she get in? I swear I checked the list and she damn well wasn't on it. I'm so sorry. I'll get security onto her." Stephanie frantically grabbed for her earpiece, pushing everything else that was on the table onto the floor.

"No, leave her alone. I don't want to draw any attention to her. She can't do any harm. Anyone that talks to her knows what they're in for."

"But what if she slurs the book?" Stephanie said, seeming agitated that she wasn't in control.

"Don't worry about that. She's not here for the book. She's after celebrity gossip and has come to the wrong place. She's the least of our worries – look who's over there." As I pointed to Henry Dent from *The New York Times* Stephanie sounded like she was on the brink of an orgasm.

"Oh my God, oh my God, wait until Hilary knows that he's

here. Oh my God, I just can't believe it. Oh my God."

"It's not that great if he doesn't like what he's read Stephanie."

"Oh come on, Alice, he wouldn't be here unless he liked the book."

"That's not true. He's been known to turn up at a book launch, appear impressed, and then pull apart the book."

"I think you'll find that's only happened twice. When he bothers to show up it's a sign of his respect for the author."

"You are up on your critics," I teased. "You'd hope I would be, wouldn't you?"

The launch was a bigger success than I ever expected, and seemed to move seamlessly from a night I was silently dreading into one that I didn't want to end.

When I woke up the following morning I regretted how much I had drunk. I could vaguely remember the evening, and the stench that wafted up from the lounge reminded me that the party had definitely finished off in our London apartment.

"You ok?" Mark whispered. "That was a heavy night."

"Christ, I feel awful. I think if I try and get up I'll be sick," I said, trying half-heartedly to raise my head off of the pillow.

"I knew how drunk you were when you told everyone left at the bar to come back to ours. Do you remember being at the bar?"

"I think so," I said sheepishly. "Was it me that invited everyone back?"

"Yes. It wasn't going to be me, knowing that we had to be out by 7:30."

"Why didn't you stop me? Thanks for looking out for me, we're supposed to be a bloody team," I said sarcastically.

"How could I have stopped your fun? You were having such a good time."

"I'm surprised Stephanie hasn't called in with the papers."

"She'd know better than to do that. It's only 6:00."

"Oh God, I need at least another two hours' sleep."

"Sorry, sweetheart, you need to get up. We've got to be at that production meeting in an hour and a half."

"I can't face it. Christ, my head's hurting."

"It was the shots that did it. I said to you don't do anymore but you gave me that look: the 'Alice is doing whatever she likes tonight' stare. So I let you get on with it."

"I so wish you hadn't. Have we really got to go and talk about a bloody televised book reading? It's the strangest thing I've ever been asked to do. Are people really going to sit and listen to me reading my bloody autobiography?"

"They must believe they will or you wouldn't have been asked to do it?"

"Can you imagine how boring it's going to be recording it, let alone for the people watching it?"

"Let the commissioning editor decide on that. He must believe it will work or he wouldn't be wasting his time."

"I suppose so."

"You're a familiar, warm face and people need hope and comfort now. It's not as abstract as you think."

"It's going to feel like storytime for bloody adults. I just can't see it working."

"Wait until the production meeting to see exactly what they've got in mind. I bet there's a creative spin to it."

"Can you imagine if they want to put me in front of a fire? It's going to be the most cringeworthy thing I've ever done."

As we arrived for the meeting I was surprised by how many people were sitting in the room. I couldn't resist being sarcastic. "Good morning," I said loudly making sure I caught everyone's eye. "This feels cozy. Who says entertainment's been hit badly?"

I sat down and leaned into Ben, the commissioning editor. "Are all these people really necessary? I thought we would be discussing everything privately between ourselves."

"I hope you don't mind but I wanted to get everything agreed this morning so I do need everyone here. I'm right in thinking you're willing to commit to this 100 per cent?"

"Yes, I said I'd do it, but under the provision that you'll be flexible about the recording time. It's impossible for me to commit to a bulk recording, but yes I want to work with you, if you really believe it's going to be good viewing for people?"

"People want to be uplifted and inspired and you're our answer to that, Alice. Even if they've read your book, to hear and see you actually reading it is a different matter altogether. Your interviews alone pull in audiences no one else gets close to at the moment, so yes I know it will work and yes we'll talk about the flexibility issue."

Ben went around the table introducing us to everyone. There were four of us compared to about twenty of them. Mark was sat next to me, to his left was my literary agent and to my right was my assistant, Pippa. She was brilliant at her job and filled in all the gaps where I lacked. Organization wasn't my strong point, and I was often in awe at the way she arranged and managed things. She was discreet, but knew her job and the boundaries between us.

"What we propose is that you read about five chapters per program, and to give viewers something more we end each program with an interview. You talking candidly with an interviewer discussing an aspect of the book that you would have just read out. People are always interested in hearing what you've got to say so we're very keen to run with the interviews as well."

"That sounds fine to me. At least we'll be giving people more than just the book. Who's going to do the interviewing?"

"We want to suggest Amis Moore."

"Alice is never going to have time to do the readings and be interviewed by him," Pippa interrupted.

"We'll keep him under control," Ben assured her.

"And how do you plan to do that?" I asked.

"He'll be under strict time instructions. We can put it in a contract if it makes you feel more comfortable?"

"I like Amis, but do you really think he's the right man for this?"

"Don't you think we've thought about that," sparked up a lady in the far right corner.

"I'm sure you have, but my job is to think about Alice, and we all know how long Amis likes to cross-question for. I think you'll remember how long he took when we returned from Iran. It was only out of courtesy that we let him carry on for as long as he did," Pippa said, sounding irritated.

Ben had been in the game for long enough to know that he needed to interject as quickly as possible before he was on the losing foot. "Look, Alice..."

"Pippa's got a point, Ben. Amis is a fantastic interviewer, but is he really right for this? Isn't his time better spent grilling politicians?"

"I know what you're saying, but the combination of you and him on TV is definitely a winner, Alice."

"So how much extra time are you asking for? Surely you're about to double the time we originally agreed to?" Pippa asked.

"We want to run a 10-week series for an hour and a half a week. We'll dedicate an hour to the book and half an hour to the interview. Ideally we want to do all the interviews in one hit. We'll decide with Amis the questions and then he'll fire them at you, Alice, over a day. Would you be happy to get all the interviews done in one day?"

"I'd rather do it in a day if you really think it will work with Amis? I'm willing to give it go."

The conversation went on for another two hours and by the end we had agreed to go ahead with the program with Amis being the interviewer.

We left the meeting and headed to the countryside to spend some valuable time with our children. I felt humbled to have such amazingly supportive parents and as far as the boys were concerned, Grandma and Grandpa's house was their home too. They loved being there and when Mark and I had to be away in London, or abroad I never felt like we were compromising their childhood by them staying with my parents. On the contrary, they gained so much from being around two people who loved them as much as we did, perhaps giving them far more attention than we could ever afford. We never talked about the boys publically and kept them out of the limelight in an attempt to keep their lives private, which meant that time apart from them was inevitable. I couldn't wait to see them and knew our time together would go too quickly.

A few days of rest and fun felt like hours and before we knew it we were saying goodbye to the boys to start another week of book-launch mania.

Within three hours I was back in London and heading to the hotel in Knightsbridge to meet Amis. He really was a man of many words and I knew it was in my interest to stick to his questions and not deviate in any way. We had always got on well in the past but I couldn't help thinking he was better suited to a subject matter much meatier than I could offer him today.

As I reached our hotel suite I couldn't help noticing a very obvious 'no smoking' sign on the door. Yet it hadn't stopped Amis from lightning up the moment he had arrived – the smell of smoke hit me as soon as he opened the door. It wasn't unusual for journalists to completely ignore the rules when it came to smoking. I knew he would rather pay the fine than spend the day going backwards and forwards outside in the cold.

Amis made a point of saying how tired he felt from spending the best part of the last few weeks in the halls of Westminster and how much he was looking forward to our day together. We spent some time catching up, mostly on matters not relating to our task at hand, and then being the true professional it wasn't long before he was firing questions at me. Although he was normally very serious, today we managed to have a few laughs and I felt relaxed answering everything he was asking me.

"Ok, Alice, I've got a question that I wish I could broadcast on TV, but I know I can't. But let me ask you anyway?"

"Go ahead?" I said, unsure what to expect.

"Why do you talk about sex so much? The sex scenes in your autobiography totally stunned me. It's like you're this politically incensed, change-the-world do-gooder, who's completely and utterly obsessed with sex."

"Can't say I've ever been summed up like that before, Amis. Why can't this be a valid question that you can broadcast?"

"Oh come on, Alice, can you imagine the corporation allowing me to air that?"

"Why can't you bloody well ask me about sex? What's the big deal? Everyone's obsessed with it in one way or another?"

"In nearly every print interview when you're asked about the secret behind your relationship with Mark you always talk about the great sex you have. Sometimes you make it sound like that's what bonds you."

"It is, well it's certainly one of the main things that keeps us so loving towards one another."

"I think this is really what the nation wants to know – why do you and Mark look so in love with each other, despite how much work the pair of you do together?"

"Mark and I are a team in every sense. I know it sounds corny but it's true. Whether we're working together, or in bed together we're always trying to do the best for one and other. That's why I love sex so much. It's such a physical way of feeling close to him. I love the emotional intimacy that we share, but our physical bond is explosive."

"Thanks, Alice. The way you replied to that I might actually be able to use it."

# III

# The Book Tour (from Alice's perspective)
# A week later...

It had been a long, hard week and I was starting to regret that
I'd ever agreed to the book tour. Everywhere we went people
wanted interviews. Most of the questions were the same and
I was starting to bore myself by my repetitive answers. Yet I
loved meeting the people who came to the book signings, and
always enjoyed hearing about what they thought of the book. I
hadn't agreed to the autobiography to see three hundred pages
written all about me. Yes I wanted the publicity for our cause but
also desperately wanted people to realize that like many of them
I had experienced the dark night of the soul, been pulled through
life's toughest challenges, and as a result had found meaning to
it all.

I took a deep breath and got ready for the first ten interviews
of the day. A tall, grey-haired man, very smartly dressed, entered
the room. I hadn't met him before and I had a feeling he would
be more cynical than most.

"Good morning. Have you been offered a drink?" I said.

"Yes, but I'd rather just get down to business. Do you mind if
I start straight away – I know the time limits that are on me?"

"Of course. Fire away."

"The book seems to start quite late in your life and then goes
backwards. I think it works but it's not the normal format for an
autobiography. Is there a reason why you decided to write it like
that?"

"Honestly, it wasn't my decision. My editor decided it would
work best that way."

"The book's written as if you wrote a diary. Did you?"

"I started journaling when I first admitted to myself that I was suffering from depression and needed to get help. I found it easier to write down how I was feeling than speak about it at the beginning. After that I kept writing, virtually every day for years. Somehow it helped me make sense of everything that had gone on and gave me the impetus to push through and deal with it all."

"So you took a lot of the book from your diaries?"

"Look I've got nothing to hide. I was interviewed by a journalist, my ghost writer, for four intensive days and then afterwards I realized that everything she wanted to know I already had written down. It was a very difficult decision for me to pass over my diaries, but I finally decided to let her into my innermost thoughts."

"So you didn't write the book yourself?"

"Technically, no, but I can assure you that the majority of it was taken verbatim from my diaries. Please don't think you've got a great scoop. It's the messages of the book that matter, and yes every one of them and their experiences is wholly legitimate."

He didn't take long with his questions and I couldn't help thinking he would make a major issue out of the fact that I hadn't written the book myself – it hadn't really occurred to me that it mattered.

You always had to expect at least one interviewer to ask about a completely different subject, and the lady who entered next didn't even try to pretend she was interested in my autobiography.

"In an interview you gave a few months ago you talked about how we all have a choice. To fold under the pressure of the current economic crisis and fight for survival or realize there's another way to live. What you said was deep and profound and hard to digest. Please can you expand on it."

"I'd love to, but the people who are paying for me to talk to you won't be happy if I waste their budget on anything other than talking about the book. Let's arrange a time to speak in a few weeks."

Having been a journalist myself I knew her tactics, and she kept pressing, wanting me to answer her questions, but I knew I couldn't answer them. I'd already riled the publicity team by admitting I hadn't written the book and now Stephanie was hovering over me like a hawk. "If you're not going to ask Alice about the book please leave," Stephanie interrupted.

"I need to know more about Alice for the review I'm writing."

"I think you'll find the book says enough," Stephanie said rudely.

"Look, give me your details and I'll get in touch with you," I said trying to diffuse the situation.

"Fine," she said and walked out.

Stephanie could be fierce when she wanted to be and for the rest of the afternoon I felt like I was being watched over by an overbearing school prefect.

Arriving back at our apartment after a very long day, I finally had time to flick through all the press clippings from the book launch. I couldn't help noticing how each one was surrounded by stories of doom and gloom. Virtually every page spoke of the dire situation we were in, from the latest company collapses and general economic meltdown, to sweeping commentaries about doomsday scenarios. It was as if the papers were preaching a warning foretelling Armageddon and I felt angry that they were painting such a bleak picture. Yes, we were experiencing a depression but they were encouraging a further decline. Why was it that the newspaper industry worked on such sick cycles? Violence supposedly sold and so pages had been dedicated for years to scenes of hatred and cruelty. The bigger and sicker the crime, the greater coverage it received. Now sadly a new wave of copy was forcing itself into the collective consciousness of the country – the end of time was being propagated everywhere and the media was doing its hardest to create as much panic as possible. I knew now, more than ever, that it was the right time to take Clive up on his offer.

Poor old Clive always got the brunt of my outbursts. He was one of the most respected owners in the publishing industry and someone I could call a very good friend. He believed in what we were doing, and over time had given us more column inches than any other newspaper group. He had approached me to write a column for his national paper, but at the time I had said no. Now I wanted to make it my priority. I called him in the hope that it wasn't too late.

"Hi, Clive, I know I'm seeing you tomorrow but I want to run something by you. I'm ready to write that column if you'll still have me? I want to start showing people there's a way out of this mess and madness. It's time to try and change people's perceptions. This fear is crippling everyone and everything."

"Come on, Alice, no one wants to hear about false hope at a time like this?"

"It's not false, Clive. We're at an evolutionary leap and people need to adapt and change to the new era we're moving into. If they don't they're going to suffer greatly and it doesn't need to be like that."

"For fuck's sake, Alice. You and your fucking prophecies. You seriously think you're going to be able to write about God's plan for humanity at a time like this?"

"That's not what I'm saying. Don't underestimate people's faith, Clive – more people than ever before are turning to religion and searching for meaning to their life. Millions of people believe in a higher power. From the paper's point of view there's a market for spiritual discussion. This isn't about 'my God's better than yours', it's about individual's discovering their direct connection and the life-changing inner peace that brings."

"Alice, if we start on all that God stuff we'll just alienate all the fucking readers. No one wants to hear about God at the moment.

All we'll get is thousands of fucking angry letters?"

"Let the debate at least have a voice and let me make a promise to answer every letter."

"What are you after, Saint Alice? To lead the people to fucking salvation? You scare me with your fucking delusions. We're in the middle of a fucking depression and you want to start writing about God and his great plan."

"That's not what I'm saying, Clive, and you know it. You aren't the only national. I'll go to someone else and get them to listen to me."

"You know I'll back you on every cause you want me to, but what you're asking is too fucking much from me."

"It'll be your loss, Clive. You wait and see."

"Babe, call me before you leave for Iran, I still want that scoop – have we still got a deal?"

"Yeah, we've got a deal, but you've pissed me off with your lack of faith in me."

"For fuck's sake, Alice, this isn't about you, it's about me not letting you use the paper to try to convince people they have a way out of the shit they're in. You sound like you're mad when you start talking like this."

"Christ, haven't you had enough evidence to see that it's not just me. Last week you said there were now too many people all thinking and believing the same thing – that you couldn't ignore it anymore. You've got the goddamn chance to be at the forefront of change and you won't do anything about it. You make me so angry. All that power at your goddamn fingertips wasted."

"Come on, Alice, don't talk to me like that. You're fucking impossible sometimes, do you know that?"

"Am I really asking too much of you? Where's your bloody conscience? Isn't there a part of you that feels bad for what the media's doing to people?"

"So you're trying the guilt trip on me now? Why won't you ever take no for a fucking answer?"

"For the same reasons that you won't, Clive."

"Right, I'm promising you nothing, nothing at all but I'll give you the chance to send me a mock-up of what you're talking about."

"I *love* you. I won't let you down. I'll get it across to you as soon as I can. See you tomorrow."

It was a week before I could get anything to Clive, but as promised he received an example of what I had in mind. He called within an hour surprised by how tame it was.

"What do you mean tame? What did you think I was going to write? Give me some credit, Clive."

"Stupid me for thinking otherwise, but I thought it was gonna be along the lines of some our late-night conversations."

"Do me a favor, Clive, it's one thing what I say to you, and another to the bloody nation. I'm not putting myself forward as a bloody spiritual teacher – I'm just trying to give people hope and the option to think outside the box. By the way, within three months you'll have a double-page spread dedicated to a spiritual teacher who will boost your figures beyond anything you can imagine now. It's what the people need and you're going to give it to them."

"Christ, Alice, you and your fucking predictions. I hate it when you say things like that because it gets me thinking."

"But you don't believe, Clive, so why would you think about it?"

"Oh, piss off and start writing your column. We'll run a teaser this weekend and go live the following Sunday."

"Thank you so much. Love you. I'll call you before we leave for Iran."

I put the phone down to Clive and was immediately drawn to the television. We hardly ever watched the news but for some reason Mark had decided to put it on, although he was nowhere to be seen. I stared in disbelief at what I was seeing.

"Damn them. The bastards have gone and done it. Come and look at this," I said to Mark as he walked back into the room.

"Christ, it's exactly how you saw it."

We sat watching buildings being brought to rubble, as smoke imploded onto the screen in front of us. The ticker that ran along the bottom of the television ensured that we could be in no doubt – we were at war.

We were both gripped watching the news as the phone started ringing. I had a feeling it would be Clive, and ran to answer it.

"Alice, have you seen the fucking news?"

"I'm watching it now."

"Fuck me, it's just how you said it would be. Is this really about needing a fucking war?"

"You know it is, Clive. Call Milton and get those documents. He'll do anything for you to print them."

"Christ, I'm gonna put the paper on the line if we print those. We'll never get another government interview again."

"I know how much I piss you off pushing you with all this shit but someone's got to start telling people the truth. Anyway, the government needs you more than you need them. Would it really hurt for them to go elsewhere for a while? You'll come out tops as the truth teller in the end."

"I told you if I saw the images for myself then I'd back you, Alice. The fucking problem is I didn't believe it would ever happen."

"It's happening all right. I wish it wasn't but it is. Within an hour Graham can get you whoever you want to speak out about what's going on. This isn't about me, Clive – this is about the goddamn truth. Just give me the go ahead and you can make bloody history. Everyone's waiting, they just need a platform to reach the people."

"Where does your energy come from? Don't you just want to resign yourself to the sad fact that we're entering into another war and there's not a fucking thing we can do about it."

"We can stop it. There's enough people who want change, who've had enough of war. You've got to believe it. I know it's not going to happen overnight but we can't give up now. Come on, Clive, put your bloody neck on the line and tell people the truth."

"Christ, I've just realized you were supposed to be in Iran next week?"

"That's the beauty, I'm still going. Everything's set up. We'll be able to get Jenny in so she can film. It's all very well for a few of us to know what's really going on but that's not going to bring about change. We've got to fight now. We've got to get the truth out."

"And face being fucking assassinated? Alice, there's a part of me that's too old for this shit. I just want to get on with my job, not start a bloody crusade."

"Will you honestly be able to live with yourself, knowing the truth and doing nothing about it?"

"This is a fucking huge decision for me to make. If I'm going to back you, I want someone imbedded with you in Iran. We can't take this stance in the paper and then contradict ourselves on the TV station. If I'm really gonna commit to you and your fucking band of merry men then I've got to do it across the board. Do you know what I'll be doing for you if I agree to this?"

"You're not doing it for me, Clive. Do it because you've seen the evidence and know what's really going on. Do it because you really give a shit. Not for me."

"Do you know what? For the first time in my fucking life I'm going to take a huge risk. I'm with you, baby, they can't keep getting away with this shit. I'm going to Whitehall to speak to Jerry. He's got to be given the heads up so he knows the line we're gonna take from the start. Gonna warn him who we're going for – give him a chance to step down."

"I forgot about Jerry. They'll force his resignation when they find out."

"You know this could be the greatest thing the paper ever did? If I die for this I might even go down as a fucking martyr. Imagine that – Clive Lanson, the fucking martyr?"

"Don't start looking over your shoulder just yet, Clive. But once you go live you know you'll be protected."

As the war raged, so did the campaign to get the truth out. Whilst the pro-war propaganda got stronger and stronger, the growing voice of dissent worked hard to disprove its lies. The more they tried to justify the war, the more people spoke out about what was really going on – and as a consequence, cries of a huge conspiracy rang through virtually every sound bite the government and those closely associated gave. Yet it wasn't enough to silence the momentum that was building.

Within three weeks over fifteen cabinet ministers had resigned, and many who had at first hailed the war as a justified action were now turning their back on it. The biggest blow to the war effort came after we released footage and pictures of the atrocities that were really going on behind the scenes. What we had witnessed for ourselves no one would have believed unless they saw the proof for themselves. It was unfathomable to think that village after village was literally being vaporized. Each one in less than ten minutes – yet as far as the rest of the world was concerned this war was targeting specific terrorist groups. It was unthinkable that the real victims were innocent civilians trying to get on with their lives. This was genocide on an unprecedented scale. A plan so highly developed and executed so quickly that millions could be wiped out and made to disappear within minutes.

# IV

# A long-awaited reunion

As Simon waved from across the room I started to make my way over to him. Although it was packed with people his height gave him the advantage and made it much easier for me to spot him. It had been over a year since we'd seen each other and I couldn't wait to be in his company again.

As I got closer to him, pushing my way through the crowd, I could see how tired he looked. He had been busy directing a film that had taken him to fifteen different locations in seven months, yet despite his grueling schedule he still found the time to help us. He was one of our most influential ambassadors and when time permitted was now our main spokesperson. Whenever he spoke, he always commanded a huge audience and the press loved him for it. As a result we were always guaranteed great publicity, which was important for us. We needed his influence for funding and to keep the pressure up on the respective governments that we had to work alongside – although mostly worked against – but we weren't looking for any kind of revolution, as had been suggested at the beginning. We stood for making change for the better. We held people accountable and cut through PR bullshit to get solutions solved to problems rather than just talking about them.

Simon had the courage of a warrior and never took no for an answer. He believed it was about solving one problem at a time and often spoke out about injustices and how things could be done differently. His ability to fund raise was mind blowing – alone he had raised nearly a billion dollars for our projects in the Middle East.

"It's so good to see you, Alice. It's been too long," he said as we hugged each other.

"I know. How are you, you must be so tired?"

"I've definitely been better – haven't slept in three days. I'm exhausted to be honest."

"Why? What's happened?"

"We're way behind schedule. I shouldn't be here tonight but it was too tempting not to come. I've called a break for everyone. We start back at the studio at 6:00 and hopefully it will start to come together. It's been living hell this one. The logistics are a nightmare and we're already onto our second producer. Do you remember Nigel? He quit last week, so that was stress I didn't need. I think I'm getting too old for all this shit. Let me retire and come and work full time for you?"

"You'll have to take a pay cut but the job's waiting for you, sweetheart."

"Can we talk in private, there's something I'm really concerned about?" he said quietly. "We can go upstairs?"

I followed his lead as we removed ourselves from the crowd and made our way to a quiet room upstairs.

"It's about Iran; I've got a serious concern about the whole thing. If we're really going to do this then we need to demand a change. It's worked everywhere else – let's pressure them now before you go in."

"Sweetheart, it's done. Graham met with the deputy chief last week and he's made it clear that we don't step foot on their soil unless the legislation has gone through and been approved. They can't let us down now, it would be diplomatic suicide. Anyway, remember we've got Abdul on the inside and everything's been drawn up – it should be approved by Friday. It would be a goddamn miracle but we might just witness equality for women within the next few months and that in itself will be a huge feat – in a way bigger than the rebuild."

"That's great news. I'll call Graham later. I've been out of the loop on this one, but I'm not rushing into another film. Going to take some time out."

"Damn, there's never enough time to talk properly. Mark and I are going for something to eat later, do you want to join us?"

"Yep, would love to. If you haven't booked anywhere let's go to Livie's, I haven't been there for ages."

"Ok let's meet out the front at 10:00."

"I'll be bringing someone with me who you're going to love to meet."

# PART TWO

The Autobiography of Alice Bailey

This book is dedicated to Mark, for teaching me to trust and being my catalyst for finding what was always hidden within me

# Acknowledgments

First and foremost I want to acknowledge everyone who believes in peace. Peace through non-violence, rather than the peace we've been sold. To all those amazing souls who have fought to find peace within themselves, and then the world. A huge thank you to everyone involved in the publication of this book. A special thanks to Pippa for picking up the pieces, all the time. To Clive for his immense support and putting his neck on the line, time after time. Aaron and Simon for their tireless efforts for change and everyone else who dedicates so many hours to help our cause without expecting anything in return. And a big thank you to all my teachers along the way. At the time I may not have liked the many lessons that you taught me, but I realize now where they were leading me.

# FROM ALPHA TO OMEGA

# CHAPTER ONE

The beach was beautiful – more serene and peaceful than I had ever expected it to be. The waves lapped the sand and protruded so quickly, as if they were being made to leave the shore as fast as they arrived. The color was hard to describe. Turquoise probably gives the best indication, but that isn't giving the myriad of colors the description they deserved. Imagine five different shades of turquoise all woven together, and then as the sun hit a certain point those colors changing into a further five different shades of blue.

I could go on describing the sea and the beauty that was before me, but my attention wasn't really on the natural state of my surroundings. For the first time in over two hours I became aware of the sand underneath me, and the uncomfortable feeling of having it stuck in places it shouldn't have been. But I didn't care. I had had my fill of the three S's and was reeling in how good I felt.

We sat staring at each other, still in awe of the peace that surrounded us. It really was the opportunity of a lifetime and we wanted to make the most of every minute. We talked for a while, but the urge was too strong not to embrace one another again. Being alone on a deserted island, with at least an hour before our ride home arrived was too good an opportunity to miss.

I gazed into his big brown eyes, and moved myself, so I was lying as close as possible. He turned his body to face me. I let my eyes wander from his as I looked down his body. It was so beautiful, to me more stunning than the sea before us – the contours around his stomach, his long, long legs, and his manhood in full glory. I loved every single thing about this man, and as I leaned over to kiss him, our bodies merged together.

It was if we were stuck. Barely moving, small delicate kisses continued until I moved my way down the front of him. He tried to reciprocate, but I urged him to lie back and enjoy what I was doing.

As I kissed his body, savoring every part as my lips gently caressed his skin, I thought about our amazing reunion and how our lives had been transformed as a consequence. I knew without a doubt that we would never be separated again. Our love and bond was too strong for anyone, or anything to ever come between us.

I moved myself back up to face him, and felt his hand meet my breast. His soft touch on one of the most sensitive parts of my body made me feel so sensual. How did he do it? How did he touch me in such a way that made me literally melt? It was so sensitive and caring, yet sexual all at the same time. Momentarily unable to move, I lay back enjoying being caressed by him and then gasped a small sigh of complete pleasure as his hand made way for his lips to take over loving me.

I hadn't believed it was possible to feel loved like this. Through all that I had put up with in the past – the abuse of the body that was now being adored – it had been inconceivable to imagine the situation I was now in. Sex was something I was forced to do. I was so weak at the time that I didn't believe I had a choice. Luckily, it became less and less, to the point where it was physically impossible. My body closed down – if I was going to do nothing about my situation, it certainly was. He tried many times, I cried in pain, but it was no use. I had shut down mentally, and my body wasn't going to let him in.

In dealing with that terrible time in my life, I had learnt a lot about myself, especially that I viewed sex as an agonizing experience, rather than an enjoyable one. It had taken a lot of hard work to get over those feelings, but now they were gone, the pleasure was greater than anything I had ever fantasized about.

As his fingers touched the most intimate part of me, a wave of warmth filled my entire body. I placed my hand over his, and felt the motion of his rhythmic movement intensify as my body fully surrendered to his touch. I was in heaven. I cupped his cheeks in my hands and kissed him with a passion I didn't know existed within me. The intimacy between us was electric. Yes, it was pure lust but there was something deeper, something more profound. This wasn't just about us individually feeling aroused. This was about wanting the other to feel complete pleasure. It was about fulfilling each other rather than ourselves.

He entered into me, and we both lay motionless for a few minutes, just enjoying the closeness of the moment. It was impossible to stay like that for long as the need to move with one another became too strong. We shifted ourselves so that we were sitting up, and I locked my legs around his lower back. Then, still intertwined, he lifted me up and carried me into the ocean. As we lowered into the water his eyes penetrated mine and we allowed the movement of the sea to determine our pace.

# CHAPTER TWO

It was an afternoon I would never forget. As we climbed into the sea plane I was so relaxed I found it hard to put my seat belt on, as I fumbled about trying to clip it into place. Settling into my seat I rested my head on Mark's shoulder and closed my eyes, relaxed and ready for the journey back to the mainland.

The flight was filled with bumps and stomach swirls, but despite the turbulence I managed to fall asleep. Just before we landed, Mark tried to gently wake me up, which took longer than he had anticipated. I had fallen into a deep sleep and as I opened my eyes I momentarily forgot where I was. I couldn't have picked a more perfect place to be. I sleepily exited the plane and feeling off balance stood for a few moments, still in awe of the experience we had just had.

A small boat waited to take us back to our island retreat, remote from roads and neighbors. It had been a long-awaited dream to stay somewhere so private that we could only enter or leave by boat. To some this solitude would have felt too much, but to us it was ideal. Our aim with the holiday was to avoid the press at all costs. Yes, for the past few years we had appeared on more pages of the nationals and celebrity magazines than most other people, but there was also a time and place for privacy, and we valued having time alone, without the eyes of the world upon us.

We boarded the boat and set off for our little place in paradise. It wasn't long before we had reached the boardwalk that led us back to our beautiful Caribbean cottage. With palm trees surrounding us and exotic flowers in abundance this was a unique place to be. The smells of island living were everywhere, and we stood still holding hands for a few moments taking it all in. The decking at the back of the cottage made way for a plunge pool and barbeque area that overlooked the sea.

We opened up the double doors and admired the view. Although it was tempting to sit outside, I had had enough of the sun for one day and showered in preparation for the night ahead. Even our most sacred trips away involved a few nights of being entertained.

The evening would be a formal affair, and I tossed a few different outfits onto the bed in anticipation of what to wear. I normally wore whatever I was advised to, but now that I had to make the decision by myself, I regretted that Suzie wasn't by my side. It hadn't been long since we both had a stylist, and it made us laugh that what we wore had become so significant. Whilst it was fun having a professional to put our outfits together, there was a serious side to her job. Our image was important and Suzie's genius ensured that we always looked stylish. We were color-coordinated most of the time and she often insisted that we wore complementary fabrics, which at first we were uncomfortable about, but had come to enjoy.

"I can't believe how lost I feel without Suzie," I said as I walked outside in my towel. "I know we tease her when she makes us match, but I don't know what to wear." He gave me that smile that made me feel that whatever I put on would be perfect. "Do you think it will be really formal?"

"When was the last time you were invited to a prime minister's holiday home for dinner and the evening wasn't formal?"

"I don't remember ever being invited to a prime minister's holiday home," I teased.

"Well there's a first time for everything, and you're being invited because you're you. Why don't you wear whatever feels comfortable?"

"Can you come and help me choose?" I had an ulterior motive the moment I asked for Mark's help and he knew it. He followed me into the bedroom, and watched as I pushed all my clothes onto the floor. I stood on the bed and put my arms around his neck. There was a big difference in our height and this position was perfect, with him standing on the floor and me on the bed. He undid my towel, and we started kissing. As we kissed, the phone started ringing and I opened my eyes. We looked at each other, as if we should ignore the call, but something in both of us knew we needed to answer it. Mark went to the phone, as I pulled my towel around me. Everyone had agreed to only phone us if there was an emergency. We knew the kids were ok as we had only spoken to them in the morning, and we'd both checked into the office the day before.

As Mark started to repeat what was being said to him, I sat down in disbelief that it had actually happened. He put the phone down before passing it to me, thinking I needed time to digest the information before I spoke to anyone – but he had underestimated how happy the news would make me feel.

"Sam's dead. He was found three hours ago."

"Was it suicide?"

"Yes."

I was filled with a wave of relief. He was finally out of our lives forever. I had known from the moment he was arrested it would only be a matter of time before he took his own life – and now it was a reality.

Throughout most of our relationship, people had been fooled by Sam's charisma and manipulation – but what lay behind his public persona was an uncontrollable monster. Many on the outside, who only saw the show, were shocked when I finally mustered the courage to leave him. They couldn't understand why I had left a life of opulence and luxury, turning my back on such a well-connected and wealthy man. But it's impossible for anyone to understand the truth unless you've told them the facts, and I kept most of my marriage close to my chest. There were those that knew of the abuse, had witnessed it firsthand and over time had distanced themselves from me. I came to understand their divide was out of frustration that they could do nothing for me, and could no longer watch my self-destruction.

"I just can't believe it. I feel like such a huge weight has been lifted. I really want to celebrate."

Perhaps it initially sounded cold to Mark that I wanted to rejoice in the face of Sam's misfortune, but he had brought me and others so much pain it was impossible not to see the situation as anything but sweet justice. Despite how good life had become, he was my constant reminder of how bad it had been, and now I could finally close that painful chapter in my life.

I enjoyed a silent celebration that evening. As everyone sat around a huge table admiring the prime minister's artwork, I was inwardly ecstatic about the news we had just received. I tried to pay attention to the conversation that was flying around the table, but I was in my own world realizing the huge impact Sam's death was having on me. Not that I was missing out on anything – the talk was mostly about boats, the biggest and the best, and it was boring. Perhaps it would have been interesting if you owned a boat yourself, but a large proportion of the guests had flown in from cities. As I looked around the table I noticed that half the people sitting there weren't paying any attention to what was being said either, yet the etiquette didn't allow for other conversations to be started. It was as if four people were holding court and everyone else had to just sit and listen.

At the end of the dinner we were encouraged to take our coffees to the outside bar. We walked onto a huge veranda and from there made our way along a dock that seemed to strut out far into the depths of the ocean. There was something eerie about walking above the sea at night, as each step took us further out. But as we arrived at the bar it couldn't have felt cozier, with its soft lighting and comfy seats. The decking in the middle of the seating area made way for a glass panel which was illuminated by huge underwater spotlights. The effect was stunning and we all sat staring at the beauty of the sea life below us.

Like most of those formal evenings, the men and women tended to separate, and it was mostly women who had made their way down to the dock. Although it often irritated our hosts, Mark and I always stuck together and mingled between the two parties.

Often the evening would entail being asked lots of questions and having to think on our feet as to the most diplomatic way of answering them. However, on this occasion it was a more relaxed atmosphere as we enjoyed chatting about the beauty of the Virgin Islands, before making our way back to the house and politely making our exit.

All I could think about was Sam when I closed my eyes that evening. He was the last person I wanted to focus on, but however hard I tried I couldn't switch off from him. I lay awake thinking about how our relationship had been doomed from the start – yet I hadn't allowed myself to see it. Our marriage had physically ended years before I actually left him, and had never really started emotionally. It was impossible to be close to someone who used emotional manipulation in every way they could. How I had then let it to get to the point of violence seemed insane, but at the time I had lost the very essence of who I was. My self-esteem was so low that I was incapable of believing I deserved better than the situation I had found myself in.

For a long time I had justified Sam's behavior as a result of mental illness, and had been determined to stick by him. It was the only explanation I could find to try and make sense out of the terrible way he behaved. As a result of convincing myself that he was ill, I had taken on the illusory role of caring for him, believing his actions were the result of something he couldn't control. I started to think that the more I did for him the better the situation would become. Of course, the more I did, the more he expected, and as his demands increased so did his aggression and contempt for me. It took a long time for me to realize it was actually me who was ill allowing him to act the way he did, without making him take responsibility for his actions towards me.

So much had gone on that I could now put to rest, and I knew the relief my family would be feeling. From the moment I had met Sam it was as if a hurricane had torn through the harmony of my family life in England, and left devastating results. Being a control freak and realizing close family and friends posed as a threat, he had been determined to cut me off from them. But what had been obvious to those on the receiving end of his manipulation, I was unable to see. A family member once described him as amoral to which I had taken great offence, yet over time I had come to realize that it was true – he really didn't have a conscience.

Denial is a powerful thing and life can seem so much sweeter if you don't allow yourself to see the truth – and so in admitting to myself that Sam had only ever used and manipulated me, I had opened up wounds that I didn't even know existed within me. It was as if it had been easier to live with his abuse and justify his actions, rather than face up to the fact that I did have a choice in getting out of the situation I was in. It seemed so insane to think now that I had normalized what went on between us, never telling anyone for years about how terrified and weak I really was.

The sun was coming up and pushing its way through the small cracks in the blinds. I felt a warm arm embrace me and rolled over to stare into the most beautiful eyes in the world. They literally sparkled as they gazed back at me.

"I can't sleep," I said.

"I know."

How was it possible to feel so loved and secure when only years before I had felt that my entire world was ending? How life had changed so dramatically for the better.

# CHAPTER THREE

We were at the airport waiting to board the plane and were sad to be leaving. It had been the best holiday ever, in more ways than the break itself. As we reminisced about our short time away we were spotted by a reporter equipped with her camera. However much we tried to hide, it just seemed impossible for a newspaper not to get wind of where we were.

I recognized Isabelle as soon as she got close to us. It was hard not to notice her long blonde hair, puppy dog blue eyes and glamor-model figure that initially fooled many an unsuspecting interviewee – yet today she looked understated compared to her usual turn out.

"Don't worry, there isn't anywhere I can run and hide. Go on, ask away," I said reluctantly as she approached us.

"Hi, Alice, I promise I'll be quick. Just ten minutes that's all – you know what I'm going to ask you? Do you mind talking about Sam?"

"No. It just seems odd that you've come all this way to ask me about him."

"I was in Florida when Patricia called and told me find you. It only took me 30 minutes to get here."

"I hope it's worth it for you. Fire away."

"How do you feel about Sam's suicide? Do you think it was the result of him knowing he would be found guilty?"

She had planned her questions and kept firing them at me. If it wasn't for the respect I had for her we would have walked away long before she had finished her inquisition – but I stayed and answered her questions as honestly as I could. I had learnt that honesty was always the best policy when it came to answering journalists – no matter what the outcome.

"Sam's sister was interviewed by one of our staff reporters

this morning and she said she hadn't spoken to him in over seven years. She openly admitted that she had decided back then never to see him again, but wouldn't say why. I know you're not going to tell me the reason, but had they always had a bad relationship?"

"Look, the long and the short of it is that Sam had far more enemies than friends. It was one of the reasons why we moved to St Kitts, other than the obvious tax benefits. He managed to keep up such a façade for so long, but the truth always comes out in the end? Just for the record, he had cut himself off from his family way before they gave up on him."

"You must have been devastated when it was reported that Sam had allegedly murdered Sonia Burns?"

"It's so tragic that it eats away at me all the time. I still find it hard to accept that he was capable of killing someone. I'm just so grateful I got away from him when I did, but I often think about Sonia and what she must have gone through."

"I'm guessing you went through a lot yourself when you were married to Sam, but understand you don't want to talk about it."

"No, it's not something I want to go into now."

Sam's funeral was a strange affair. I had my writer's hat on as I observed the reactions and behavior of those who attended. The only people who were truly sad about his death were those that hadn't known him long. It was as if everyone else had been expecting it for years. I felt really peaceful and found myself saying a silent, sarcastic thank you to him across his grave – although it was more an acknowledgment to myself that as a result of the awful times we had spent together I had found an inner strength and drive that I believed wouldn't have surfaced without all the suffering.

My main concern that day was for Archie and George. Even though they hadn't seen their father for over three years, he was still their dad and I expected them to be upset as they came to terms with the reality that they would never see him again.

Archie had disconnected from Sam way before his death, and I knew it would be easier on him, but was surprised when he asked if he could now call Mark his dad. I had always believed that Archie saw in Mark all the qualities that he couldn't find in his father, but had never expected him to embrace Mark so fully. Mark adored both the boys and after hearing Archie's comment asked if he could adopt them.

I was filled with happiness as the positive repercussions of Sam's death played out in front of me. They say that blood is thicker than water, but I learnt that day that genuine love is the bonding factor between two people, not necessarily the blood that links them.

The gathering back at Sam's mother's house felt a bit like being in a Mike Leigh film. Everyone was supposed to be sad, but somehow couldn't put on the show. I overheard a close friend of the family saying that he had always believed Sam would either become a multi-millionaire or end up in prison. His predictions couldn't have been more accurate, although they were both short-lived. Sam had made a fortune, but a few huge gambling mistakes had put pay to a large amount of his savings. He had also spent two weeks in jail when he was first arrested. Taking his life had prevented his predicted twenty-year prison sentence.

We left early and I vowed not to waste another minute thinking about Sam. All my attention was now on my new family. 'New' in the sense that Mark was about to officially become the father of my two children. Over the previous few years it had felt like he was their father, but today I realized the reality. We asked both the boys if they were ok and if they understood what had happened. We wanted them to be comfortable that they could talk to us about how they were feeling. We tried as best we could to explain the situation and sat speechless as George, the younger of the two asked: "Did Daddy fly to God?"

We sat in silence both desperately trying to think of how to answer him.

"How did he get to God, Mummy? Did he fly or did God come and pick him up? God won't take me will he?"

It was one of those moments that you wish you'd been given a manual for. How to answer a child without ruining their innocence was one of the hardest things about being a parent and we were both stumped, unsure what to say. We tried as best we could to answer him, but he was obviously confused about death and we weren't sure we had helped him in any way.

George spent the night in our bed and it ended up with him sleeping soundly and me being awake. A recurring nightmare stopped me from sleeping. Every time I closed my eyes I saw a knife literally flying through the air and piercing me hard on my shoulder as I moved to try and protect my body from the onslaught. It was something that had actually happened when I was married to Sam, and it was obvious that the day's events had unleashed memories I was trying hard to suppress. Perhaps I needed to talk more about all that had gone on, but I really didn't want to waste any more energy on the past. As I lay awake, frightened to shut my eyes, I wondered if I was just putting off the inevitable? Was it really possible to pretend traumatic things didn't happen by trying to forget about them? Did it help anyway to relive them by remembering them? I knew it had helped years ago in finding the strength to leave Sam, but now he was gone I wished the memories would just disappear.

I felt strange waking up the following day. It was the early afternoon and I was stunned that I had slept for so long. Not that it mattered – everything had been taken care of – the children were at school and the house felt calm. I was met with my usual morning cup of tea, and a hug that made for the best start to the day. If I could I would have spent all day in those gorgeous arms, but the day called and there was work to get on with. I still couldn't believe I had slept for so long. How things had changed. Turn back the clock and either the kids would have been running riot or I would have been screamed at to wake up.

I sat in front of my computer and stared at the screen. I logged onto the office server but it was no use, I just couldn't find the motivation to do any work. I thought about the passion of the past few days, the idyllic island we had left behind, and looked around at the beautiful setting we now lived in. I loved the house so much, and living in the country suited all of us, and made for a very happy environment. But today I wasn't feeling my usual positive self. It was as if a cloud had set in that I couldn't move from above me.

Mark was in the garden practicing a speech he was giving in the evening. I walked outside and sat quietly listening to him. He had such an amazing way of commanding an audience. I often thought it was due to his presence alone, as he had the ability to silence a room just by standing in front of everyone. He was the leading authority in his field and I was so proud of how successful he had become. I loved the passion in his eyes as he spoke from the heart, and knew it would go down as another hugely defining evening. He stopped talking and looked at me.

"I feel so strange," I said, not really knowing how I felt, but needing to say something.

"Do you want to talk about it?"

"I don't think I've got over everything that went on with Sam. I hate the fact that I'm still thinking about him. I just want to get rid of the memories. I don't want to waste another minute talking about it."

I turned around and walked back inside and sat at my computer. Mark followed me inside and put his arm around my shoulder. His warm touch triggered floods of tears. I just couldn't stop. I cried and cried, and as I did he hugged me. It was as if I had been bottling them up for so long, and the lid had popped, and out they rained. It had been a long time since I'd allowed myself a good cry and as a result I felt like a huge weight had been lifted.

The crying fit certainly didn't deaden my passion and as Mark and I started to kiss, I realized how safe and loved I felt. I allowed myself to feel completely vulnerable and needy towards a man I knew only wanted the best for me. Perhaps until this point I had never acknowledged how traumatized I actually was regarding all that had gone on with Sam. From the moment I had left him I went into survival mode, which didn't allow for me to wallow on what had actually gone on and how painful the situation had been. It felt better that way and helped me to feel stronger. Of course, the memories would rise up, reminding me of how weak and manipulated I had been, but I consciously pushed them to the back of my mind putting my 'happy bubble' in their place. It was a trick I'd read about in how to deal with unwanted thoughts and feelings, and perhaps to a psychologist it was obvious that what I had tried to do would inevitably catch up with me. Somehow I knew deep down that my outward persona was covering up an inner turmoil that I didn't want to go near, let alone confront. It was a pain that reminded me of all the aspects of myself that I felt ashamed about.

# CHAPTER FOUR

Things started to settle after Sam's funeral – for the children anyway. They seemed remarkably ok and I kept waiting for their fallout. It was me who was affected more than anyone else.

Day by day my positive thinking started to be erased, literally inch by inch, as negative thoughts crept in trying to convince me that I was only really the sum of a weak and broken women fooling myself into who I thought I had become and showing myself to be. Yes, I knew deep down that without a doubt the hardest time of my life living with Sam had actually turned out to be the making of me, but I still felt completely out of control and fearful about the way I was feeling inside.

Foggy was probably the best way to describe how I felt every morning for at least a week when I opened my eyes. Nothing was clear, there was haze around everything I looked at. When people spoke to me I pretended that I was listening, when really I wasn't. Not because I didn't want to. My mind was all over the place and it was difficult to hear what was being said to me. As far as doing anything public – that was a no go until I got myself together. I had become a pillar of strength, yet was anything but. I felt like I was letting down the very people that were looking to me for inspiration. It was a harsh lesson in remembering the very thing I was trying to remind others about – our thoughts really did affect the way we felt.

Not wanting to allow myself to wallow anymore I decided to take back control of my thinking. Whenever a negative thought popped into my head about Sam I consciously changed it. I couldn't let myself believe what my mind was trying to convince me of. I knew I was different now and my outer life reflected that truth. It was time to see my life in St Kitts from a different perspective – it certainly hadn't been all doom and gloom – far from it. I had made some amazing friends, and owed so much to one person in particular – Nathan White, the unexpected voice of reason when things got too much for me to handle. We had become friends through an unusual set of circumstances resulting in him single-handedly helping me to get away from Sam. We had enjoyed a close friendship, but a mistake on my part meant that we were no longer in contact with one another.

I had always felt lifted when we were together in St Kitts and able to handle the nightmare I had to return home to. I would leave Nathan after having lunch together, mostly every week, and then not want to go home. I always paused as I put the key in my front door, frightened by what I would meet as I walked into the house. As I opened the door I invariably felt my body shake, but my children were inside and I looked forward to seeing them. They were my motivating factor for staying with Sam at that time in my life – alongside the fact that I was absolutely terrified of him.

On one particular afternoon the front door flung open before I'd even reached it. Sam was livid as usual when he had been left for a few hours with the boys. His usual immaculately styled blond hair was ruffled as if he'd been violently pushing his hands through it, and his frosty grey eyes pierced mine as he glared at me.

"It's fucking 3:30. You said you'd be back by 3:00, you bitch." As he spoke, he lurched forward, inches from me. He did this often in an attempt to intimate me – sometimes going further. On this particular day I knew that's what he had in mind. I moved back thinking that he was going to try and hurt me, which he did, but failing to hit me he grabbed my arm instead and pulled me forward – so hard that I lost my balance and fell to the floor. His rage was the result of having been left with his children for over two hours. He saw his weekends as time for him and his mates and resented being asked to look after them. I'd seen nothing wrong in him spending two hours with the children he had hardly seen in nearly three weeks, but he was mad that I had even asked him, let alone gone ahead and actually left him with them.

As I got up from the floor, Archie, our oldest boy, came outside to see what was going on. Sam was stood looking at me with contempt, but moved backwards as he saw Archie coming towards us.

"Come here, sweetheart, have you had a fun afternoon?" I said to Archie, trying to sound upbeat as I hugged him. It was the familiar feeling of trying to fight back tears, wishing everything was so different.

That evening was a defining one in our relationship, and whilst harsh, was the start of my road to recovery and a time that I felt proud of. After I'd put the children to bed, shaking I tried to explain to Sam that his shouting and violence towards me had to stop. But as I spoke, literally standing up for myself for the first time in our relationship, Sam's face became wild with fury. Lines that I'd never noticed before protruded from every angle and his eyes suddenly looked too big for their sockets. There had only been a handful of times when I believed Sam had actually wanted to kill me and this was one of them. Yet somehow I wasn't frightened of him. The meek and subservient side of me had given way to an inner strength that allowed me to finally stand up for myself. It felt so good.

"How dare you blame me. If you weren't such a bitch I wouldn't need to scream at you." For the first time I heard the absurdity of what he was saying to me. Before I had felt guilty, believing that I had somehow pushed him into behaving the way he did towards me – but not today. Something snapped in me and I screamed back at him.

"Stop it, how dare you speak to me like that. How dare you." I walked away from him into our bedroom, slamming the door behind me. No sooner had it closed, then it was flung open again and as it did the bottom of the door hit me hard in the back of my left ankle. I tried to block the door from opening but the pain was instant and I had to move out of the way. There was a moment of silence and I thought Sam had retracted back into the lounge satisfied that he had at least hurt me. But as I bent down to see if I was bleeding I knew he was there – just on the other side of the door frame but close enough to grab my hair. He pulled hard on my ponytail, pulling me down. He was holding on so tightly that my neck was forced backwards as he tugged harder trying to yank me to the ground. I always had two choices in those situations – to make it worse by trying to fight back or go inwards and wish it would stop by avoiding more confrontation. I always chose the latter.

"Look at me, you bitch. Don't you ever, ever walk away from me again. Who do you think you are? Don't you dare storm off like that."

As he let go of his grip on me the strength I had mustered in walking away from him waned, and I found myself slumped in a heap crying on the floor. I felt so helpless, but showing emotion always made him angrier.

"There you go trying to get my sympathy. You're fucking pathetic. Do you know that?"

He grabbed my arm trying to force me to stand up.

"Get away from me," I said, so quietly he could hardly hear me.

"Get up," he shouted.

"Please be quiet," I said, trying to hold back from crying even more. "The kids are asleep."

"You should have thought about that before you acted like this. Get up. Get off the fucking floor. You're pathetic."

"If you try and hurt me I'll call the police," I said, surprised that I'd actually said it. It was something I had never dared to say before and he knew I meant it. He moved away from me and made his way towards the door to leave the room.

"You'll regret that threat. Don't come anywhere near me

tomorrow, and don't ever, ever threaten me again. I don't want to see your fucking face anywhere near me; do you hear me, you piece of shit?"

He slammed the door and within seconds George started crying. I went to comfort him.

"It's ok, sweetheart," I whispered as I leant over his cot and started to stroke his hair. I'm not sure who I was really reassuring – perhaps I was speaking to myself more than him. I cuddled him for a few minutes and then tucked him back in. I closed the door and went back into our bedroom.

I wanted to sleep in the spare room, but knew it would only inflame the situation, so I stayed awake all night, frightened of what Sam might do. I hated more than ever that Sam and I worked together, made all the more difficult by the fact that Sam was my boss.

At work the following day I could sense how uncomfortable everyone in the office felt as he deliberately tried to reduce me to tears from the moment I entered the building. It was as if everyone around me, just by their body language alone, was trying to say to me to just walk out – but Sam paid their wages and nobody was going to take the risk of betraying him by standing up for me. Silence reigned throughout the morning as everyone pretended to get on with their work, trying to act oblivious to what was obviously going on between us. The most uncomfortable point came when Sam decided to shout at me across the office. It was open plan and humiliating that everyone could hear him.

"What were you thinking when you wrote this? This is shit. Don't bother to do it again. I'll get someone else to write it. I don't know why I thought you could write – you can't."

I knew there was no one else in the office who could write for him. He was trying to provoke me, but I kept silent and said nothing.

Throughout the morning he tried similar tactics but I wasn't going to let him get the better of me in front of everyone. After lunch, I walked up to his desk and said very discreetly that I was leaving for the day – something I had never done before. I had had enough and couldn't handle an afternoon like the morning.

Sam let me walk out of the office and then ran after me. I was about to get into my car when I heard him shout across the car park.

"Wait, don't go, Alice."

I knew he wouldn't make the mistake of trying to hurt me in front of anyone, so I shouted back.

"Stay away from me. I've had enough."

"Don't you dare get into the car."

"Go back to your office, Sam," I shouted, praying that he would stay where he was.

"Don't ever walk out of the office like that again. Now everyone will think they can just leave when they want to. How dare you fucking leave when you've got work to do."

"I've had enough of you talking to me like that. It's best I go home. I'll be back tomorrow, and if you treat me the same as today then I'll leave again." As I heard myself speak I was proud of how I sounded.

"Get back in the office. Don't you dare just go."

I was frightened of the consequences but knew I had to drive away. I got in the car, locked the doors, and left as quickly as possible. I looked in my mirror and saw him light a cigarette. It was the first time I had ever walked out during the day. I was scared how Sam would return in the evening, but knew I was right to finally stand up for myself.

I got home and memorized the number for the local police station – just in case I needed it, and phoned Nathan. Just hearing his voice was normally enough to help me relax – but I never mentioned to him what went on with Sam. I felt like a fraud for not being honest with him, but I was too scared to tell him the truth about my relationship.

When Sam came home that evening he was calmer and started to act as if nothing had happened during the day. The cynical side of me knew what that meant – he wanted something from me. Normally he wouldn't have spoken to me for at least a week, apart from in the office, but today he was different and attempted to make conversation. It was easier in some respects when he refused to speak to me, at least the house was quiet and I wasn't living in fear that he would try and hurt me.

I was outside taking long lugs on a cigarette, when Sam put his head around the back door and tried to sound friendly.

"We've been invited to the British consulate for dinner tomorrow night. Can you take my suit to the dry-cleaners and make sure it's ready for tomorrow evening?"

I hated the confrontation and disharmony that went with his terrible temper and so, feeling comforted that the screaming had at least temporarily stopped, agreed to do it for him. There was also another reason why he had decided to talk to me.

"Something urgent came up today that I need you to work on. We've got to submit a dossier by close of play tomorrow. Can you have a look at it? It would be better if you could write it tonight, so I've got time to read it tomorrow."

I was stunned by what he asked me. Any sane person would have told him where to shove his dossier, but frail from his abuse I reluctantly agreed, relieved that a recurrence of the previous night's behavior had been avoided.

As I typed away at the computer until late into the night I realized how stupid I had become. I craved for calm in the house literally at any cost, which was why previously I had never stood up to Sam. I had taught him that he could treat me as he liked and then as soon as he spoke in a nice way I was putty in his hands. How ridiculous I had let the situation get.

# CHAPTER FIVE

I had made a mistake thinking that my initial show of strength with Sam would last. It couldn't. Not unless I was prepared to leave him – which I wasn't. The few weeks that followed were hell. But whilst I had shown myself that I could be strong – the outcome was the opposite and I grew weaker around Sam, doing everything I could to avoid a repeat of the events that occurred as a result of my standing up to him. It got so bad between us that on more than one occasion I found myself retreating to the bathroom, working out a way to cover up the physical signs that would have shown everyone the truth of Sam's violence towards me. Had I not been so insecure I would have told someone about what was going on between us, but I was too frightened to tell anyone. Irrational, yes, but at the time it felt like the only thing I could do.

Life carried on like a rollercoaster for what felt like years. There were some good times, but overall it was an awful, painful part of my life. Friends came and went, and my family had to pull away. They had tried all they could to talk sense into me, but I became too defensive and they knew they couldn't get through to me. I continued to see Nathan, just as a friend, and went through all the confusion of how I felt for him. When we were together life was great. He made me feel so good about myself, but it was only temporary and by the time I got home I felt helpless again. It helped that we started to meet more often – which I never had to hide from Sam. Due to his huge ego he never once suspected that I had feelings for Nathan. In fact it was the opposite – he couldn't imagine Nathan being attractive to anyone – let alone me. He always referred to him with contempt – Nathan wasn't cool enough, or part of the right set for Sam to welcome him into his world, and as a result he never saw him as a threat. Nathan's wife didn't suspect anything either, most probably because he had a handful of close friends that were women. The trust must have been strong between them and she often invited me to events that she had arranged. Sometimes I thought it suited her that I was there and Nathan wasn't sitting in a corner getting bored. She was a socialite through and through, whereas he was happy to sit on the side, and would do anything to avoid small talk.

During this period I fought with feelings that got stronger every time I had to leave Nathan. Most of our conversations were focused on our similar interests, and predominately his newfound passion for becoming a therapist. It was a subject close to my heart and I found it fascinating that he had turned his back on a career as a lawyer to study alternative therapies. I respected him for making such a drastic career change late on in his life, and started to witness changes in the man I had become so close to. He seemed more comfortable within himself, and was so much more fun to be around – a newfound playfulness he attributed to finally doing something he was passionate about.

Whenever Sam came up in our conversations I presented an image of a very happy family. Part of me longed so much for it to be true that I enjoyed giving the impression that I was content and all was well. Those that had an idea of the truth had distanced themselves from me anyway, and I was desperate not to lose Nathan too. So I painted a picture that everything was good between Sam and I – an image that extended to our social life as well. Sam had all the bravado and could convince anyone that I was his adored wife when he wanted to. But amongst his friends it was an in-joke that as long as their wives toed the line, everything would be just fine. It was an attitude that spanned across his whole clan of island mates – to the point where whenever 'the boys' talked about their wives, it was always with contempt.

If I hadn't moved from England to live in St Kitts I believe I would have left my marriage much sooner than I did – but I was cut off on an island with only a few people who I could call a close friend. There was so much pretense and people were far more interested in how much money you had and what you could do for them, than wanting a genuine friendship. As the days went on I regretted more and more that we'd moved to St Kitts. Home was England and I was desperate to return there. It had been a huge mistake for me to leave. Sam had convinced me it would be good for us, but I hadn't wanted to go. As usual I allowed myself to be bullied into agreeing to it, instinctively knowing it wasn't right for me but not being able to cope with the confrontation that went with not agreeing to something Sam wanted to do.

Somehow once we arrived I assured myself that everything would be different between us, living in the Caribbean and being surrounded by luxury. The perks seemed amazing and even my family and friends were taken in with the lifestyle I was to enjoy. There was the huge house, swimming pool and boat docked at the end of the garden, with a twenty-four-hour captain on call. A full-time cook and housekeeper, and a nanny lined up to help with the children before they were even born. Sam had even leased himself a helicopter and planned to visit as many islands as possible. I thought I was to be included in his days out, but I was to learn that this was something only him and the boys did together. God I hated 'the boys'. Individually they were ok, but together they were like pack animals, always on the hunt for the next best thing. They believed they were better than most other people and looked down on those they didn't let into their inner-circle. It was clear to anyone close to them that over the years they had brought out the worst in each other.

I gradually started to bond with some of the other wives whilst the boys were on their 'away days', and often ended up at Julia's house. She was my favorite out of the 'ex-pat wives', and our children were similar ages, which helped with us making friends. I was often at her house with the boys – especially when Sam and her husband were out together – which they weren't supposed to be on this particular occasion, but had gone regardless of the arrangement I had made with Sam. We'd agreed that he'd spend a few hours with the boys, but at the last minute he announced that he had to be somewhere else and left the house and the boys wondering where their dad had gone. I don't know why I didn't learn – and made the decision that day that I wouldn't allow Sam to let them down again. I would no longer rely on Sam to spend time with them.

I had never mentioned to Julia about what went on with Sam but I couldn't keep my anger back when I went over to her house that day. Her penthouse towered above the shoreline of the east of the island and offered fantastic views – the clear glass lift to get there gave an added perspective allowing for a sight of virtually the whole island. The added bonus that the lift slowed down at each floor and then sped up again, was always the highlight of our outings to Julia's house. The boys loved the way the lift jolted from one floor to the other and then held their breath as it slowed down before taking off again. The delight on their faces was worth the additional times that I had to go up and down with them, before eventually arriving at her door.

I could always guarantee that a drink would be waiting for me when I arrived – and it was never just one. I knew deep down that we were both looking for an escape when we got together. Her playroom kept the kids busy for hours which gave us the benefit of drink and chat time.

"I'm so bloody mad with Sam, he's let the kids down again," I said as we walked onto her veranda, not wanting to give too much away but needing to vent. She followed me out and placed a big jug of Pimm's onto the corner of a table that was big enough to seat about twenty people, and we slumped into two immaculate large leather cream chairs that looked like they'd never been sat on.

"Aren't you used to it?" she said sounding surprised. "Doesn't he do it all the time? I know Larry does."

"Why do we put up with it?" I asked as I took a large gulp of my drink.

"For this," she said, as she stood up and took a photo off of the table which she kissed and put back down. It was a picture of their huge yacht which was moored at the local harbor.

"If it wasn't for Larry I would be living in a small house, living a dull life, and would never have known how fun it could be to have all this."

The more she spoke the more I realized she had it all sorted out in her mind. Larry meant material gain, and there was an obvious distinct lack of love in anything she said. It started to sound like she really hated him and I wondered if he behaved with her in a similar way to how Sam treated me. Although she didn't give much away about their relationship, I started to suspect that we had more in common than I had first thought.

"Whenever I try and talk to Larry about spending more time together he just gets angry with me, so I've given up. I cope with our relationship by always looking at what it's given me."

She had come to the point of justifying their relationship in terms of things rather than her and him and I felt sad that we were both in such loveless marriages. From an outsider's point of view we had everything, but we were both empty inside, wishing things could be different. Perhaps Julia could cover up her hurt of Larry's rejection by loving everything she had around her and wanting more – but I came to the stark realization that afternoon that I was desperately lacking the very thing I really wanted from life. I craved to be genuinely in love and be loved back – all the wealth in the world could never have meant more.

# CHAPTER SIX

I became more and more depressed living in St Kitts. The initial dream of a life in paradise was being shattered by the day, and as the weeks dragged on I prayed that I would find the strength to leave Sam. Of course there was no denying that my surroundings weren't spectacular. The sun beamed most days and the sea sparkled as if millions of little stars danced upon it. But it had been a long time since I had allowed myself to see the beauty that others appreciated – I was in a dark place that even the brightest sky couldn't lift me out of.

I kept up my meetings with Nathan, and always had an urge to tell him the truth about my relationship with Sam, but found myself keeping quiet about the very subject I needed to talk about. I was too scared to utter a word to anyone. It was as if a seal of silence had been cast over my lips and I couldn't break its hold over me.

It was an afternoon after a particularly difficult week with Sam when Nathan asked me what seemed like a simple question. As I heard his voice on the telephone my heart raced with excitement about what he might say.

"Alice, please will you be my guinea pig?" he said in his usual over polite way. "I would be so grateful for your help for the final module of my degree. Would it be possible for you to meet me at the beach tomorrow around 9:00 and I'll explain what I need you to do?"

It wasn't what I was expecting and I jumped at the chance to meet him at the beach.

The following day couldn't have come quick enough. The sky was clear and the sun bright as I opened the door for the first time that day. The air conditioning inside the house always gave a false sense of the real temperature outside, and whilst I was met with a surge of heat as I stepped outside, nothing prepared me for the temperature inside the car. Literally within seconds I was sweating. I opened all the windows but that made no difference at all. I closed them and waited for the cold air to circulate throughout the car. I hoped the beach would offer the wind that was lacking inland, and looked forward to feeling the sea breeze.

I watched Nathan sitting on the beach as I parked in a spot that allowed me to walk straight onto the sand. I closed the door of the car quietly, not wanting to disturb what looked like him meditating. He was sat with his legs crossed and back straight facing the sea, wearing his customary white linen trousers and white short-sleeved shirt. I thought about how creased his trousers would look when he stood up, and how much that would upset him. He couldn't bear looking untidy, almost to the point of obsession and was always immaculately turned out. He was a small, toned man. His white clothing emphasized his year-round deep tan, which looked unnaturally dark compared to his auburn colorings. He was a handsome man by all accounts, but not in the traditional sense.

"Hi," I said quietly, seeing that his eyes were open but feeling uncomfortable about disturbing him.

"Great to see you, Alice, thank you so much for coming down," he said in his soft Canadian voice, that could easily have been mistaken for a mid-west America accent, and often was much to his disgust.

"I want you to help me with a few experiments. Nothing too challenging, in fact all I really need you to do is relax, and I'll do the rest."

It was easy for him to suggest, but relaxing wasn't something that came naturally to me and I immediately felt tense just thinking about it. In truth it wasn't something I knew how to do. It seemed ridiculous that sitting on the beach, staring at one of the most beautiful sights in the world couldn't have the effect of helping me to slow down my mind and make me feel at ease.

"I'm not sure how to relax," I admitted, feeling stupid.

"That's not a problem, I'll lead you. All I want you to do is lie down and close your eyes."

It felt strange but I told myself I had nothing to lose. I was internally adamant that what he wanted to do wouldn't work on me but I had to give it go, for no other reason than it gave us extra time together. I lay flat on my back, and tried to let my body sink into the towel beneath me. I stared up at the sky, but the brightness of the sun only allowed me to look for a few moments. I shut my eyes and tried to concentrate on his voice. It seemed bizarre what he was asking me. I had to focus on my toes, then my legs and then he headed upwards directing my attention to what felt like every limb of my body. Although my mind kept wandering I was desperate to try and concentrate on what he was saying, and the more I listened the more I found myself relaxing.

As his voice moved through the different parts of me, so did a wave of relaxation that I'd never felt before. I could feel the towel beneath me, but my body started to feel weightless. My mind was quiet and the usual worries and fears started to disappear. I was in awe of what he could do. As I allowed myself the luxury of listening intently to what he was saying I realized what a soothing, deep, sexy voice he actually had. I became transfixed on the sexiness of his voice and for a few moments fantasized that he was lying next to me telling me how much he loved me. I imagined his face directly above mine as I watched him move closer towards me kissing my lips in a gentle, but passionate way.

"Alice, are you awake? Can you hear me?"

"I jerked as his voice brought me back to reality. It had seemed so real but I quickly realized it wasn't. I felt cheated. "

"Alice?"

"Yes, I'm awake," I said quietly, wishing I wasn't.

"You were in deep thought, can you tell me what you were thinking about?"

Of course I couldn't. Panic set in as to how I was going to answer him. How could I tell the truth that I was thinking about him? My heart started racing as I thought about what I should say.

"Don't be shy," he said, trying to encourage me to speak. I stayed silent unsure how to respond.

"It's ok, this is all part of the experiment I'm trying to prove. You don't have to feel self-conscious, just say whatever comes into your head."

*Come on, come on,* I said to myself trying to think of something to say. The pressure to make something up was overwhelming.

Before I had had a chance to vet how I was going to answer, I said something – literally without thinking. "I hate myself."

I was stunned by what had come out of my mouth. Nathan was silent and I wanted the sand to swallow me up. I knew it wasn't the answer he was expecting and couldn't believe I had said it. He lowered his tone and I felt him move closer to me.

"What made you say that?"

"I don't know."

I tried to stay silent but a force I couldn't control was pushing, urging me to say more.

"I've lost most of my friends and family, I'm in an abusive relationship and I'm not doing a damn thing about any of it. I feel totally out of control. I hate my life. If it wasn't for the children I don't know what I would have done by now. I'm shit scared of Sam. I've got myself into something I can't get out of."

He was shocked. His little experiment had brought up far more than he had bargained for, and I had spoken for the first time the truth about how I was feeling.

"You weren't expecting that were you?" I said, embarrassed and hopeful that I could break the intensity of the moment. I opened my eyes and saw him staring at me. I closed them quickly and waited for him to speak.

"But I thought..." He stopped and didn't carry on. There was an awkward silence. "I thought you were happy, you always seemed so happy?"

"I've been putting on a front and pretending to be happy."

I felt foolish for having been so dishonest with him and knew I'd let him down. I felt worse than ever and hated the way I had lied to him. The words that Sam had often said to me rang through my head. I really was a lying, conniving bitch. I had manipulated my relationship with Nathan pretending to be someone I wasn't. The confident, happy persona that I had projected about myself couldn't have been further from the truth. Perhaps the right circumstance had never arisen for me to tell Nathan the truth, but I knew I wouldn't have done anyway. He must have felt like he didn't know me after all the time we had spent together.

My eyes were still closed when I felt his hand touch my leg, in a warm affectionate way.

"I want to try something," he said. "Please keep your eyes closed and let me relax you again." I tried to follow his lead and literally within minutes felt relaxed again.

"Imagine Sam is standing directly in front of you. You're protected and can say anything you like to him. He can't answer you back or react in any way – he just has to listen to you. Are you ok to do that? Can you start to tell him exactly how you feel?"

I tried to digest what he was asking me and as strange as it seemed I wanted to try. But a few minutes went by and I started to feel ashamed that I couldn't translate the words I had in my head. Even though I logically knew that there could be no comeback, and that Sam couldn't hear me, it was impossible for me to say out loud what I really felt. Something in me was too frightened to start speaking.

"I just can't do it," I said after an uncomfortable silence between us.

"Don't give up so quickly. Work with me. Let me try and help you."

Suddenly I felt like I was offering him far more mileage than any of his text books could afford him. I was a live case study of someone who clearly had so many issues. I felt stupid for being so worried about what I would say and tried to let myself feel safe and let go of controlling how I would answer.

I don't know if it was something that Nathan said or my determination not to feel like a failure that forced me to start speaking, but as I did I couldn't stop. What started off as a rant, ended with so much emotion that I found it difficult to keep talking. My body shook as I cried and cried trying hard to continue speaking. The sun was beating down on my body but I felt freezing inside as I tried to control the emotion that was taking its hold on me.

Nathan listened for what seemed like hours and then when I felt I couldn't say anymore I opened my eyes and winced at how much brighter the day had become. I knew as I stared up at the sky in that moment that something had shifted within me. Although I had felt so vulnerable in opening up to Nathan, now a part of me felt freer just by having spoken the words of feeling like a prisoner.

"Thank you," I said, unsure of what else to say as I sat up feeling surprisingly relaxed.

He stared at me and put his arm around my shoulder.

"I love you," he said, in a way that I knew he meant only as a friend. But it didn't matter. I felt safer than I'd ever felt before. "Please will you let me try and help you?"

I knew him helping me meant having to be more honest, and just the thought of it made me feel uncomfortable. But I wanted to spend more time with Nathan, and if that meant allowing him into my innermost thoughts and feelings, it was a price I was happy to pay.

"Yes, if you really believe you can help me, then I'd love to give it go."

"Ok, if it suits you let's meet on Tuesday at the same time, but come to my house instead and we'll do some further exploration."

A text from Sam told me that he was working late that evening, and I instantly felt relieved. After I put the boys to bed, I poured myself a large glass of wine and ran a bath. I lit some candles and stood for a few moments watching them flicker from side to side, as the wind coming through the open window took control of their movements. I found the sound of the running water soothing as I immersed myself in the bath. I took a gulp of wine, turned off the taps and lay back and shut my eyes.

It was the first time I had ever fallen asleep in the bath. In hindsight it was a good sign that I was starting to relax, but I was shocked that I had been able to fall into such a deep sleep.

I jumped up and grabbed my towel. I looked at my watch – it was 12:15. I had been asleep for over four hours. I dried myself and crept into our bedroom, but there was no need to be quiet. The curtains were still open and the bed was empty. I walked into the living room, checked the study and realized that Sam wasn't home. He often worked late, beyond the time that I went to bed, but I had always assumed he was in before now. I tried to call him but his phone was switched off.

I got into bed but stayed awake waiting for Sam to come home. Thoughts whirled through my head, from wondering if he was having an affair, to the worst possible conclusion that something more sinister had happened to him. The thought of him with another woman made me feel sick, yet the idea that something really serious might have occurred gave me comfort. My honest hope was that something had happened to him, something that meant I would never have to see him again.

# CHAPTER SEVEN

I was genuinely disappointed when I woke up to find Sam lying next to me. I asked him what time he had come home and his answer didn't surprise me.

"Not too late. It was a busy night, lots to get through. Why do you care anyway? You know I've got loads to do at the moment."

"What time were you back?" I knew I sounded confrontational but somehow I didn't care.

"Are you looking for an argument, Alice? Don't start first thing in the morning."

"What time did you get back? I just want to know."

"Christ, what's wrong with you? I didn't look at my watch. I don't know the exact fucking time." He was getting angry and I knew I had to be careful not to push him too much more.

"An estimate will do," I said sarcastically, rolling over to the face the wall.

"For fuck's sake, aren't there more important things to worry about than the time I came home. It was about 11:00. There – will that shut you up or are you gunning for a row?"

What an idiot I had been. Although I had no proof, I knew without doubt he was seeing someone else.

Believing that Sam was having an affair worked as a strange catalyst for me. Instead of feeling more depressed it made me feel stronger and want to take control. I started to admit to myself what a fool I had been for letting him treat me so badly. I knew with Nathan's help it was finally time to confront the situation and get out of the hell I had found myself in.

My next meeting with Nathan was a more formal affair. It was at his house, in a spare room that made way for a makeshift therapy room. It was strange sitting in front of him talking honestly about

myself for the second time within a week. We talked for a while –
him asking me how I felt after our time on the beach and me
filling him in on my suspicions about Sam's affair. He seemed to
skirt over the issue of Sam's affair, not really wanting to talk about
it. I felt annoyed that it wasn't more important to him but went
along with answering his questions anyway.

"If you don't mind me asking, has Sam been abusive to you
during the last week?" he asked in his usual polite way making
no reference to Sam's suspected affair.

"No he hasn't, but it's as if we're living separate lives. There's
hardly any interaction between us, but I prefer it that way.
Whenever we do talk it always ends in him screaming at me. I've
decided it's better to stay out of his way as much as possible."

"That must be putting pressure on you working together?"

"I hate it. I can't stand walking into the office every day."

"You used to love your job, didn't you?"

"Sorry, that's another thing I haven't been honest about. I hate
what I'm doing, I hate it that Sam's my boss."

"Please don't think I'm being unfair in saying this, but why
are you continuing to do something you obviously don't want to
do?"

"I've tried to leave so many times but every time I bring it up
with Sam he gets really angry with me. He always says that the
business is our future that he needs me and that I would be
letting him down. He'd have to pay someone a fortune for what I
do, and has always said that the business couldn't afford it. That
I'd be turning my back on the very thing that's allowing us to
enjoy the lifestyle we lead."

As I spoke I realized what a doormat I had become. I had
allowed Sam to use me for his own gain. It had never been about
me, it was always about what he wanted. I had let him manipulate me into believing I would be letting him down if I walked
away from the business, and in doing so had never stood up for
what I wanted to do.

"Have you always worked closely together?"

"Yes – unfortunately."

"Has the relationship always been this one-sided, or were you strong when you first got together?"

I thought back to the person I used to be before I met Sam. I was bubbly, happy go-lucky, and always tried to find the positive outcome in almost all situations. I had lots of friends and a family that adored me. Overall life was fun and I was happy. Of course I'd had my fair share of ups and downs but nothing compared to what I had experienced with Sam.

"Yes, I was strong when I first met Sam. I would never have accepted then what I put up with now."

"I want you to lie on the couch. Imagine it's the most comfy bed you've ever laid on and close your eyes."

I did what I was told and started to feel the same relaxation I had experienced on the beach. This time I was asked to imagine that I was walking in a forest. From there I was told to imagine a field full of my favorite flowers. I saw sunflowers everywhere, they were brighter than normal and taller than me, and I was surprised that I could so easily picture them. His voice led me to an enclosure, just past the field, and I was asked to imagine Sam standing in front of me.

"Can you see him?" Nathan asked.

"No, I can't," I said without really trying. The last person I wanted to picture when I was feeling relaxed was Sam.

"Would you prefer to create a symbol for him rather than trying to physically picture him?"

It seemed strange that I was being asked to see Sam as a symbol. It's not something that I'd ever thought about before and quite honestly found the suggestion weird, but it felt better not to have to see Sam whilst I was trying to relax so I tried to give it a go.

"Yes, but what sort of thing do you mean?"

"Ok, imagine a symbol that could represent Sam."

I tried hard to think of something but nothing came to my

mind. It was harder than I thought.

"Sorry, but I'm finding this really difficult."

"Ok, if you had to think of an image that represented Sam what would it be? It could be anything from a bottle of beer to an animal?"

I'm not sure why, but the symbol that sprang to mind was Taz, the Tasmanian Devil. I was familiar with his face from Archie's fascination with the TV program, and it felt fitting that Sam would now become Taz. I was told to tell Taz one thing that I wanted to get off of my chest. I thought for a moment. I knew there was so much I wanted to say, but couldn't pinpoint the most poignant.

"I'm not sure," I said.

"Ok, let me help you. I'm going to count to ten. When I say ten, tell me the first thing that comes into your mind...seven, eight, nine, ten."

"You have never loved me and I don't think I've ever loved you."

"Ok, that's great. Now I want you to turn over on your stomach and let the symbol disappear from your mind."

I turned around and felt uncomfortable as my face buried into his sofa.

"You don't look comfortable," he said, sounding puzzled as to how to make me feel more at ease. "Ok, let's try something else. Keep your eyes closed and sit up with your back towards me."

I followed his direction and got into position. I could hear him fumbling around behind me. A few moments later I inhaled a waft of smoke that smelt like an incense stick being burned. "I'm not going to touch your skin, I'm going to work above it, just let me do a bit of oriental magic."

"I'm all yours," I said, meaning a lot more than he realized. I tried to focus on the amazing smell that was literally filling the air throughout the room, but my mind was wandering, thinking how incredibly intimate it felt having him so close to me.

# CHAPTER EIGHT

It felt strange to be at the same charity dinner as Nathan and his wife. It was the first time I had seen him socially since effectively becoming his patient. He was sat at a table near the back of the room and I made my way over to see him. It normally didn't matter that Nathan and I chatted in front of his wife, after all she had invited me to many a social occasion for the purpose of keeping Nathan company. But tonight our conversation felt stilted. It was obvious a small barrier had gone up between us. I felt self-conscious that he knew so much about me, and it seemed he was having difficulty talking to me too.

I said goodbye and headed back to my table feeling confused by what had just happened. I was now Nathan's patient, and our relationship was changing as a result. I felt more vulnerable than ever and wished I'd never opened up to him. I was scared that he might say something to his wife and knew she wasn't one for keeping secrets. I wanted our old way of being with each other back and felt ashamed that I'd told him too much. It was too frightening to think about what could happen if Sam found out.

I sat back down at my table, shaken and wishing I wasn't there. I knew I couldn't cope with small talk so I sat listening to the conversations going on around me, conscious that my hand shook every time I lifted my glass. I was also trying to ignore the pressure that was building in my chest, and the feeling that I was moments away from fainting. Most people on our table were too self-absorbed to notice that I was having a full-blown panic attack. In an attempt to try and control my internal chaos I sat focusing my attention on a woman sitting opposite Sam, wondering if she was the reason for his late-night returns. Sam was talking loudly, taking command of all other conversations going on around the table and I watched her looking at him seeming in awe of everything he was saying. I definitely saw their eyes lock on more than one occasion. There was an undeniable chemistry between them. I couldn't sit any longer. I needed to be away from everyone. I had to go home.

"I'm really not feeling well, I'm going to have to go home," I whispered to Sam.

"For Christ sake, Alice, stay until the dinner's finished. What are you trying to do, make a stand because we're out with my friends?"

It was true we were out with 'his friends' but within the group I had forged a few friendships that Sam had tried hard to keep me away from. He didn't mind us talking when we were all together, but wouldn't agree to me going out with them alone. But his obsession with trying to keep Diamond and I apart was on a different scale. We actually had little in common, but his irrational behavior towards us even talking to one another became the very reason why we bonded.

Diamond was sat directly opposite me and although most women hated her, I had grown fond of her over time. Her name alone turned most people off but I enjoyed her company, albeit in small doses. On the surface it seemed like all she cared about was how to make herself look richer and younger, but her shallow image disguised the fun-loving, caring person beneath it. Diamond obviously wasn't her real name but a nickname given to her by her husband, which had become the only name she was ever referred to by.

As I looked at her, trying to weigh up whether to just walk out or wait, a quiet conversation between her and her husband got louder and louder, to the point where it was impossible not to hear what they were saying.

"Don't you dare call me your princess if you're not going to treat me like one," she said loudly enough to catch the attention of the people on the next table.

"Not now, Diamond," he replied, throwing his napkin onto the table.

"But you promised we'd go tomorrow."

"Leave it out, we can go on Monday?"

There was always a rush when it came to Diamond buying the latest must-have piece of jewelry.

"Howard, we need to go in the morning, I want to wear that necklace for the concert tomorrow night."

"You don't need to wear it you want to wear it. You've got a million others to choose from. Leave it out, Diamond, I mean it."

"You're making me nervous, Howard. What's happened to the man that always wanted to spoil me?"

"I said not now. Damn it, don't make me lose my temper."

It was obvious to everyone around the table that Howard had a temper that Diamond was frightened of. She quickly retreated from the conversation not wanting to push him further, but a bad atmosphere had been created and it seemed like the right time to make my exit. I knew in going home I was going to make Sam angry and allow him the freedom to be unfaithful – but I had done my time staying out just because Sam wanted me to. I needed to be at home and away from everyone.

# CHAPTER NINE

It was impossible to sleep. My head whirled, switching between thoughts about Sam finding about all that I had said to Nathan to Sam's affair. I was more paranoid than ever and convinced that I knew who Sam was seeing. I wondered who else knew.

Most married couples on the island had affairs – it seemed to be a natural consequence of looking for a way out of the monotony that came with island living. Swinging and women's only parties were also a normal part of an evening's entertainment for a lot of people. Yes, it was something that went on everywhere but it was more pronounced on an island that was so small, magnified by of all the gossip that surrounded it. It often felt like we were living in a void in the middle of the sea, where normal rules didn't apply – an island playground for the rich and famous, or for those who were running away from something. There was no stability and the community was transient. As people arrived, you knew they would either love or hate it, but most were forced by circumstance to leave within a few years of arriving. Some left as a natural result of a work contract ending, whilst others returned for more drastic reasons. It was common for a couple to arrive full of enthusiasm for their new life together, and leave as a result of their break-up.

Being away from family and close friends took its toll on the ex-pat community. It was hard to be so far away from the people you loved, made all the more difficult if you had children. We all lacked the support of having close family at hand and it was something that I longed for. It had been over a year since I had had any contact with my family in England and I was desperate to cement the relationship that had previously been so strong. They had been right all along. I had made a terrible judgment with Sam. I hadn't been blinded by love, but by lifestyle. I had bought into the belief that a lavish way of living would make me happy. Now I resented everything that was around me. It came at too high a cost – a cost I was no longer prepared to put up with.

As I lay awake, my mind racing, it became even more obvious that my opinion or what I wanted had never had a place in our relationship. It was only ever about what was right for Sam, and as a result over the years I had actually started to lack my own opinion, always giving in to what Sam thought or wanted.

It needed to be another night of induced sleep and I grabbed for my tin hidden in my side table. Over the years I had come to the conclusion that a mixture of sleeping tablets was more effective than just one. It did make for more challenging mornings but meant that I got some sleep rather than being awake all night – which happened more than I wanted it to.

When I arrived at Nathan's house the following day I felt awkward that I was going to let him into the intimacy of my private thoughts and feelings, especially after seeing him the night before. I hesitated on his doorstep deciding what to do. I felt paranoid about saying any more about my relationship and petrified that Sam would find out.

The front door opened before I had a chance to change my mind and walk away. Nathan stood greeting me with a big smile. I followed him inside. I knew the protocol and settled myself on the sofa.

"How have you been?" he asked.

"Awful." I couldn't lie. "I'm feeling much stronger though, and it's strange because I'm starting to think more about what's right for me."

"Good. That's great feedback. Have you had any more thoughts about Sam having an affair?" Nathan never held back on getting to the point as quickly as possible. He had a way of asking his questions without conveying any emotion, yet showing an understanding that went beyond what he was actually saying.

"If I could prove Sam was having an affair then it would be the perfect excuse for me to leave him. I need to work out how I can catch him."

"Why are you searching for an excuse to leave Sam when there are so many reasons that are right in front of you?"

For the first time in our friendship I felt like Nathan was judging me.

"Perhaps they're obvious to you, but it's not as simple as that. I can't just leave. There's the house, the business, the children. I don't have any money of my own; I've pushed away all my family. It's just so complicated."

"Then why does him having an affair make it any simpler?"

I was unsure how to answer him. I sat silently feeling angry inside that he was challenging me. I knew there was a sensible reason why Sam having an affair would make everything so much easier and sat thinking about how I could communicate it.

"If I can prove he's having an affair then that's a tangible reason for me to leave him."

"But then you'll be running away from the real reasons if you convince yourself that you left Sam because of his affair?" I felt a barrier go up within me. I was supposed to be feeling relaxed and he was making me feel more awkward by the minute.

"I didn't realize the reason why I left Sam was so important?"

"It's everything. Not for him, not for anyone else, but for you. You have to leave him from a position of strength, not from weakness, or it will haunt you for the rest of your life."

Somehow what he said made sense, even if I didn't fully understand what he was implying. "With my therapist's hat on I want to see you healed and then you'll have the courage to tell Sam the truth about why you want to leave him, and what to do will become more obvious."

I left Nathan that day feeling more vulnerable than ever before.

All his talk of wanting to heal me made me feel more broken. I was never going to get the courage to leave Sam. He was also too clever to ever let me find out he was having an affair and I still couldn't imagine doing it any other way.

I hurried to pick the boys up from school and spent the afternoon and early evening at the beach with their friends and respective mums. I needed an afternoon talking about trivial things – it was easy talking to people I didn't know very well and I enjoyed talking about recipes and various things that were happening on the island. I wondered how I came across to other people as I sat joining in on the conversation. I tried hard to be upbeat and chatty but thought they could probably see through me. My eyes always looked sunken and my laugh reminded me of the sound of an audience attempting to applaud an unfunny clown.

I was lying on the sofa watching the television when Sam came home drunk that evening. My aim was to wait up for him in the hope of looking through the texts on his phone once he was asleep. Realizing he was drunk, I knew it would be easy. I expected him to stagger straight into bed, but he started to come towards me.

"I'm feeling frisky," he said, as he tried to seductively undo his belt and buttons, his trousers falling to the floor. I sat up and hugged my knees into my chest praying that he would fall over from being too drunk, or turnaround and walk back into our bedroom.

"Come here," he said as he walked over to me and pulled hard on my arm.

"Please, Sam, stop it. I'm really tired. I don't want to do this now."

"You never want to do it, you little prude. When was the last time you wanted to have sex with me?" As he spoke he stared at me, whilst tightening his grip on my arm.

"Stop it, Sam, you're hurting me."

"What the fuck is wrong with you? You're such a fucking prude. You will open your fucking legs for your husband."

He was so much stronger than me. He grabbed harder on my arm and within seconds had forced me to the floor. I curled into a ball hugging my legs into my chest turning my back to him. He straddled across me and forced his elbow hard into my stomach. I cried out in pain as I instinctively held my hands into my stomach and lay on my back in an attempt to ease my agony – it hurt so much but I couldn't scream as loud as I wanted to. I was in shock. Within a split second he sat the whole weight of himself down hard on my legs, and grabbed my arms pulling them above my head.

"Get off me," I said in slow motion, with so much hatred as I tried to pull my arms away. He tightened his grip and I knew what was coming. There was a sick expression on his face as he smugly laughed at me. He enjoyed the struggle, like a cat playing with the mouse he had just caught. I felt sick as every bone in my body became rigid, and tears poured down my face.

"Try and pretend you have it in you to be someone you're not," he said, as he laid the whole weight of his body on top of me. The floor was tiled and my spine hurt as it was pressed hard into the cold surface.

Even though I was petrified of what Sam might do, I couldn't control my anger.

"I hate you. You're a sick bastard? If only people knew what you did to me. You don't deserve me, you sick bastard, get off me."

"Oh, you want to play hard ball do you?" he said as he grabbed the waistband of my trousers, forcing my knickers halfway down my legs.

With one arm free I tried to push what little nails I had hard into his back. I wanted to show him that I could stand up for myself. I also wanted to try and hurt him as much as possible in an attempt to get him off of me.

"You bitch."

He grabbed my arm and pulled it down hard against my side using his knee to hold it there, pushing my elbow hard into the floor. He eyes looked wild as he glared at me – his face inches from mine. I was terrified that he was going to hurt me. I knew I had to try and get away. I pushed my legs up as hard as I could and kicked him in the back.

He didn't even flinch.

"You want rough do you, you little whore? It's time I gave you a few lessons."

Before I had time to react I felt his fist punch hard into the most intimate, vulnerable part of me. I cried out in pain but he ignored the emotion he was stirring within me.

"You can't do this to me," I screamed.

"The more you scream the more I know you want me, you whore."

I saw his hand coming towards me and suddenly felt every nerve on the left side of my face tingle in pain by the swipe he had dealt me. I felt faint, almost like my body was giving up on me, yet I felt my heart racing, pounding through the whole of me.

"One day you'll pleasure me the way I pleasure you," he said as he attempted to force himself in me, clearly aroused by what he was doing to me. The pain was indescribable, as he tried hard to push inside me. I lay motionless on the floor frightened of what he might do.

"Open your legs wider, you bitch, I'm going to have sex with my wife."

"I hate you, you fucking bastard," I said crying and shaking uncontrollably.

He stood up and towered above me as I lay flat on the floor, too scared to move.

"What did you say, you little whore? How dare you. All I want is to have sex with my wife. It's fucking normal you know for a husband and wife to have sex."

He started to walk away from me and I lay still, watching his every move. I was sure even he'd had enough for one night and felt relief for the first time since he'd come near me. But I had underestimated his anger. He turned around, walked back over to me and screamed at me to sit on the sofa. Too weak to argue or ignore him I sat up slowly pulling myself up onto the sofa, feeling like my whole body was broken. His hand came towards my chin pushing my face backwards. He knelt on my thighs and shoved his manhood hard into my face. I kept my mouth tightly shut and wanted to bite him but I stopped myself for fear of what could come next. As he moved himself hard against me face I cried uncontrollably.

"You're pathetic. You manage to turn everything into a fucking nightmare. Don't worry, I'm not going to carry on, you couldn't turn me on even if you tried."

He walked towards the back door, lit a cigarette and slammed the door behind him.

I felt too weak to even consider leaving him that night. I lay back on the sofa hugging my legs in close to my chest, knowing that I had to get away from him.

# CHAPTER TEN

Weeks went by, that felt like months. Days merged into nights and before I knew it I was more depressed than I believed it possible to be. I walked around in a daze unsure what day it was, just about being able to go about my daily necessities. When I could I would lie in bed all day. It felt wrong but my lack of energy meant it was my only option. Thoughts whirled through my head at such a speed it was hard to make sense of anything that was going on in my mind, but mostly they were daydreams about me leaving Sam or leaving life altogether.

I had tried to keep up my weekly sessions with Nathan but it wasn't working for me. Yes, inside I felt stronger, but I seemed unable to make any physical changes and had never spoken about the horrendous night that had left me feeling more frightened of Sam than ever before. I was stuck, and what seemed to Nathan obvious moves to make, seemed impossible to me.

I thought a lot about my family in England and how I wished I could be with them. I wanted to tell them the truth about what was really going on, but the fear was too great to dare to contact them. I was so desperate to leave Sam yet everything seemed too complicated and challenging.

My children were my saving grace during that time. I would watch my oldest play and sing to himself, oblivious to the fact that I was staring at him. There was something so magical about the way he played. He showed such innocence and pleasure about the smallest of things. He was so pure, yet so knowing in a strange kind of way. As I sat watching him it dawned on me that I was learning from him without even realizing it. He was sat in front of me showing me the true secrets to a happy, fulfilled life. I was so busy mulling over the past or worrying about the future that it was impossible for me to focus on what was in front of me. I had also forgotten how to have fun. Life was so serious now and every day felt like a drudge. I was ignoring the simple things, and playfulness was something that was buried deep in my past.

As I drove to Nathan's house the following day the truth about my situation became clearer to me. I was never going to leave Sam – I was too frightened of him and what he would do to me. I was finally admitting to myself just how weak I actually was.

As Nathan opened his front door, his smile beamed right through me, emanating a warmth that felt like it was physically caressing my whole body.

I sat down on his sofa and started to cry before he had even uttered a word to me.

"What's happened? Let me get you a tissue," he said, surprised by my outburst.

"I'm at breaking point. I can't go on like this anymore. Things are worse than ever but I'm too weak-willed to ever be able to leave Sam." He was staring at me as he handed me a tissue and then sat down slowly holding eye contact.

"Please talk to me, what's happened?"

"I'm actually scared to use the words..." I said as I waffled to try and get to the point. "I'm so afraid of what he might do to me, if I tell you what I want to."

"What are you afraid of? Do you think he would physically harm you?"

"Yes."

"Has he ever hurt you before?"

"Yes." There was a deathly silence. I shook, knowing that I had just dared to speak about my deepest, darkest secret.

"I thought it was mental and emotional abuse that you have been suffering from?"

I felt like I was betraying everything inside of me by daring to tell the truth and started to regret that I had spoken. But Nathan pressed further.

"What exactly has he done to you?" I saw a change in his face. There was anger in his eyes and I suddenly felt protected. "Please open up to me, Alice. Have you ever told anyone else what you're going to tell me?"

"Never. Most people close to me have heard him scream, but the other stuff I've never dared to mention. I've been too scared to tell anyone. Anyway, I've always assumed no one would believe me, and if by some miracle they did, they certainly wouldn't be able to understand why I was still living with Sam. They'd just think I was mad."

"I don't think you're mad, I'm just starting to understand how much more complicated this is. Has he ever hit you?"

"Yes." As soon as I spoke I started to cry again, but for the first time they were tears of relief rather than sadness. Nathan sat staring at me as I sobbed, and then put his arm around me pulling me in close to him. He said nothing but his actions alone showed me how much he cared and I felt so safe being embraced by him.

"Aren't you going to ask what I've done to make him do this to me?"

"How could you think you've done something to deserve this?" It was a question he didn't want an answer for, but I knew I felt partly to blame for Sam's attacks on me.

"You mustn't go back there. You can't ever put yourself at risk again. When was the last time he physically attacked you?"

"Last night. He used to apologize, but now it's always my fault and I think I've come to believe that it's true. That perhaps I do provoke him into coming at me the way he does. I've tried every approach – including not answering back and being subservient but then it just seems to make him worse."

"You've got to leave him. Every text book tells me how I should never tell a client what to do, but this is different, you're my friend. If I don't give you my opinion I'll regret that I never helped you in the way morally I know I should do. Don't go back. Don't

be frightened of him anymore. If you're still not strong enough to
do it for you then leave him for the sake of the children."

"But where can I go? If I run to England he'll come after me,
and if I stay here he'll make my life hell. How can I get away from
him?" As I spoke I started to feel overwhelmingly protective of
the children and knew Nathan was right – I had to open up to
him more – and for their sake alone I had to get away from Sam.

"Have you thought about confronting Sam in a safe
environment and telling him you want a divorce?" Nathan asked
just as I was getting up to leave.

"I've thought about it so much, but the consequences seem too
frightening."

"If you're still not ready to leave Sam tonight then please
promise me you won't sleep in the house alone with him. I know
you're going to get the strength soon but before then is there
anyone you could invite over to stay at your house for a few
days?"

There was no one I could trust to tell them the truth, but I had
a friend who I knew would be happy to stay for the night. I
wished I never had to return home again, but the children were
there and I couldn't leave without them.

I felt calmer in the house knowing that someone else was there,
but it was difficult when Sam came home. He was still ignoring
me from the events the night before and I knew my friend sensed
something was wrong. Perhaps if he hadn't come home so early I
would have opened up to her but the situation didn't allow me to,
and we ended up drinking a bottle of wine and watching a film.
I sat staring at the pictures on the screen but my mind wasn't
aware of what was going on. I was focused on how strong I was
starting to feel – I could literally feel an inner strength rising
within me that I'd never felt before. I knew that I was changing
and finally feeling ready to leave Sam. The fact that I had
Nathan's backing meant the world to me.

# CHAPTER ELEVEN

I waited until the house was empty and called Nathan to tell him my good news – I was finally, definitely ready to leave Sam. He mimicked my enthusiasm, utterly relieved that I had finally come to my senses. He offered to set aside the afternoon and we arranged to meet at the beach. It was something we often did when we had first become friends – we would wade through the water chatting about a whole host of things, but never talking about the subject that I should have been honest about.

As soon as I arrived at the beach we got straight down to devising the plan of how I was going to leave Sam. Nathan suggested that I went to England and then told him that I wanted a divorce – but I was too scared to leave that way. I felt I had to tell him first and then get back to the UK. Nathan was adamant that I told him in a public place, where I could call upon help if I needed it. We agreed that I'd pack a suitcase for myself and the children that I'd leave in the car, and that I'd take the children to someone I trusted before I told Sam, having set up somewhere for us to run to afterwards. I decided I would tell Sam at the weekend that I wanted a divorce, having told him beforehand how unhappy I really was, to pave the way for the final blow.

As planned, the following evening would be my stepping stone to leaving Sam. We were invited to a party hosted by a mutual friend and I would use the opportunity to tell Sam some home truths in preparation for finally announcing that I wanted a divorce.

We arrived at the party together, but Sam disappeared the moment we entered the apartment. I didn't care – I wasn't ready to say what I needed to. My heart was racing and I needed to be clear about what I was going to say to him. I headed to the drinks table and then found Julia and a few other friends chatting together. I sat down with them and pretended to be listening to the conversation but really I was practicing in my head what I was going to say to Sam. When I felt ready I looked around the room to try and find him but he was nowhere to be seen. I knew I couldn't wait too much longer – I needed to speak to him before he got too drunk – I had to be sure that he would remember what I was going to say to him.

I excused myself, and glass in hand made my way to the next room. I was shaking and the nervous energy that was pulsing through my body was making me feel sick. But I felt strong, and in a strange way was actually looking forward to formally confronting Sam.

I found Sam locked within the intimidating circle of his friends and knew I'd have a difficult time getting him away from them. I walked over and confidently told him I needed to talk to him outside, expecting him to turn his back on me. Instead, he used the opportunity to joke with his friends that I was finally feeling frisky. I walked away unsure if he would follow me, but instinctively I thought he would. He wasn't used to me being assertive and I guessed that the intrigue alone would at least get me five minutes of his precious time away from the boys.

I opened the patio door and closed it behind me. Floor-to-ceiling glass windows meant that we would not be isolated outside together. Although we'd be alone, they allowed everyone inside to see exactly what was going on between us, which made me feel safer in the event that Sam lost his temper. I stared at the sea, watching fishing boats that looked like stars sparkle in the distance as I stood wondering how to start the conversation, waiting for Sam to appear.

It wasn't long before I heard him open the door. I felt an immediate tightening in my stomach as I turned around to face him.

"What the hell do you want? I only came out here to get lucky," he said as he leaned forward and tried to kiss me.

"Sit down," I said, in a voice that surprised me.

"Not now. We're at a party, don't you dare do this to me now."

"Sit down."

"Don't tell me what to do."

He turned his back on me and tried to open the patio door. I knew I needed to say something quickly before he walked away. I was shocked at how strong I felt.

"If you ever hit me again I will leave you. If you try and force me to have sex with you I will leave you, if you ever..."

I had his attention.

"Shut up, Alice. What about you? What about what you do to make me want to hit you?" he said as he turned around to face me.

"You think it's ok to justify why you hit me, don't you? It doesn't matter what I do, you twist everything. You say everything's my fault and I've believed it for so long. I've had enough, Sam. I've had enough"

"You're fucking mad, Alice, do you know that? I don't know why I'm with you. I don't respect you."

Before I had time to think about what I was saying, in the heat of the moment the words came flying out of my mouth, leaving me stunned that I had actually said them.

"I want a divorce. I'm leaving you."

"You're what? You must be fucking joking. Where will you go? You couldn't survive for one minute without me."

I knew he believed what he was saying.

"You watch me. I've had enough. Anything would be better than living with you."

"I've given you everything you've ever wanted, you ungrateful bitch." His face was inches from mine but I was determined not to feel intimidated.

"Don't you ever call me a bitch again. I'm not coming back

tonight and over the next few days I'll collect my things."

"You actually think I'm going to take notice of your threat. Here you go again trying to control me. By holding back on sex you think you can control me and now you think threats are going to work. Fuck off out of my sight."

I watched him walk inside and over to his friends and resume the conversation as if nothing had happened. I was shocked that he could see me as so pathetic that I was threatening him rather than meaning what I said. As I saw him laughing and joking it felt like I was observing a stranger, not even a human being, but a beast that I had lived with for so long. As far as I was concerned Sam was now a predator planning his next attack, and like a female bird protecting her young from the prey of a swooping eagle, I was now alert, strong and ready to stand up to him.

I left the party quietly, without telling anyone. Adrenalin was pumping fast through my body and I felt like my instincts were being heightened, in readiness to assist me. I headed for the house. By the time I reached the driveway I knew exactly what I had to do. My heart was pounding as I ran into the garage and pulled three large suitcases off the shelf. Barely able to manage two at the same time I rushed into the house with one and then followed with the others. George's bedroom was the closest so I started with his clothes. Literally pulling them off their hangers I threw them into the suitcase, and then emptied his draws. I ran into Archie's room and then panicked that Sam had followed me home. I went to the window and felt relief that I couldn't see his car, but I still felt paranoid that he could return at any minute. I grabbed Archie's clothes from his wardrobe, and then ran into my room. I wasn't really concentrating as I flung hanger after hanger into the suitcase – my priority was to get out of the house as quickly as possible. I crammed some of the boys' favorite toys into the third suitcase along with a few personal ornaments that meant a lot to me. I ran to the safe praying that the code hadn't been changed. I successfully removed our passports and birth certificates and pushed them into the bag on my shoulder. I was ready to leave. I shut the front door quietly looking around as I stepped outside and then threw the suitcases into the boot of the car as quickly as I could and stood for a moment, sweating, trying to catch my breath, thinking if I had missed anything crucial.

It was difficult to put the key in the ignition as I was shaking so much. I tried to steady my hand using my left to guide my right, and managed to start the engine. I pushed my foot down hard on the accelerator and sped away – hoping not to alert the neighbors. The houses were all set far back from the road so the chances of anyone hearing me were very remote. I knew my actions were going to have huge repercussions but I couldn't turn back or think about the consequences and headed straight for Amelia's house where the children were staying.

There was an obvious flaw in the first part of my plan and I felt panicked about what to do. Amelia's husband and Sam were friends, something I had chosen to forget until I was literally outside their house. I grabbed my phone out of my bag and scrolled down through my contacts hoping to think of someone else I could go to who wasn't part of Sam's clan. I didn't have to go far – my finger hovered over Ally's number, who lived near to Amelia. Ally and I had become quite good friends as a result of our boys being in the same class together. I didn't know what I was going to say to her but it felt safe to head towards her house nevertheless. Having never asked anyone for help before I didn't know the best way to approach her and felt uncomfortable about calling her, but acted before I had time to convince myself out of it. To my relief she answered the phone.

"Hi, Ally, it's Alice. I'm so sorry it's late, but is there any way I could pop in and see you." I felt embarrassed that I was disturbing her and didn't want to say anything more over the phone.

"It's fine, I was up anyway. What's the matter?"

"I'm so sorry to interrupt your evening. I really need to see you."

"Of course, come now. How long will you be?"

"I'm really close. I'll be with you in about five minutes."

It was good to see Ally's familiar face as she answered the door and ushered me into the kitchen, closing the door behind us.

"It's ok, Eric's away on business, and the kids are fast asleep. What the hell is the going on? You look really pale. Do you want a cup of coffee?"

"Have you got anything stronger?" I surprised myself by actually asking for what I really wanted.

"Vodka and orange?"

"Perfect."

"God, you look white. Are you sure you're ok, Alice?"

"No I'm not, I've just left Sam." There was no point in not being honest with Ally. I bit hard into the nail on my right thumb.

"Oh, my God, where are the boys? You haven't left them with Sam have you?"

"No, of course not. They're staying at Amelia's tonight but it didn't feel right to go there yet. I'm so sorry to land this on you. I'm not sure what I'm going to do."

I tried to quickly justify why I had left Sam, attempting not to make it sound like I hated him as much as I did, and not giving too much away.

"I always knew your relationship was fucked," she said, completely surprising me. I'm not sure if I was more shocked at the way she spoke, or the fact that she obviously had opinions that she had kept very quiet about. "The way you acted around him. You were so jumpy and I couldn't stand the way he spoke to you. Eric and I talked about it a while ago and he told me I mustn't interfere as it seemed like you were happy with Sam. Can I be honest with you?"

"Yes."

"I can't stand Sam. I know this could come back to bite me if you decide to go back to him, but I don't care. He's always given me the creeps. God, I can't believe you've actually left him. Eric will kill me for telling you this but the odd times when you've asked us out for dinner we've always made up an excuse because Eric can't bear being around Sam."

I couldn't believe what I was hearing. Quiet little Ally, who never said a bad word about anyone, was shocking me more with each word that came out of her mouth.

"I thought everyone loved him and that no one would be loyal to me. I'm stunned. I can't believe what you're saying."

"You'd be surprised. We've had our suspicions for a long time. I want to help you, Alice, do you need to stay here?"

"Please can I stay tonight? Oh God, I think I should get the kids. Is there any chance they can stay here too? I need to think of an excuse as to why I need to pick them up from Amelia's. It's so late, she's going to be suspicious."

"By the way, Jo hates Sam too." Jo was a mutual friend, who Ally had known for a lot longer than me.

"What? That really surprises me, he's at her house a lot."

"Not through her choice. She thinks he's a chauvinistic pig. She'll kill me for telling you that. Please don't go back to him. You'll be so much better off without him. Give me a hug."

As she put her arms around me I started crying.

"I never ever want to see him again let alone go back to him. I've been thinking about leaving him for ages but it just seemed too difficult. There's no way I'm going back to him now. I've got to go back to England – I can't stay on the island." As I spoke, I thought about how much I would miss Nathan.

"Men like him need to be in control of everything. You know you're going to have a fight on your hands but it will be worth all the grief. You've got to stay strong, girlie."

"Perhaps I shouldn't alarm Amelia tonight and leave the kids at hers?"

"But when Sam realizes you've left won't he panic and go

straight there?"

"He'll probably think I've gone mad for the night, but assume I'm coming back. If I move the boys now I think it will be a mistake."

"Have you got their passports?"

"Yes."

"That's a relief. Now, what the hell are you going to do?"

# CHAPTER TWELVE

Ally turned out to be an amazing friend. She sat talking with me for hours, helping me plan how I was going to get away from Sam. The more we spoke the more I wished I'd been honest and had opened up to her earlier. I had assumed I couldn't trust her or anyone else and kept myself trapped in my own dark world of fear and self-pity. I owed so much to Nathan. For the first time in years I felt like the fog was starting to lift from around me, and the more I talked to Ally the easier it became to see what I needed to do to stand up to Sam.

"Alice, it's easy for me to see how you got yourself into this position. He was controlling you. From what I can gather he made you believe that loyalty to him meant keeping his dark secrets. Of course, he had to be like that. He had too much to lose if you got close to anyone else and he knew that. He's far more manipulative than you realize. I can see it clearly because I'm on the outside." Ally was far wiser than I had ever given her credit for.

"I've got to phone my family in England. It's been over a year since I've spoken to my mum and dad. It's a long story but they hated Sam and I kept defending him. We eventually came to a stalemate and haven't spoken since."

The time difference was on my side. I dialed their number and waited for an answer. I was nervous and excited at the same time.

"Hello." Hearing my mum's voice brought tears to my eyes but I couldn't speak immediately because I was too scared of how she would react to me.

"Hello. Hello."

"Mum, it's me. It's Alice."

"Alice – is that really you?"

I had expected a cold reply and was surprised by the warmth

in her voice.

"I've tried to call you so many times and I've written so many letters to you. I've missed you so much. I can't believe you've called."

"Mum, I've just left Sam."

"Oh, my God. Where are you?"

She fired about twenty questions at me as if we'd only spoken a few days before, and I tried to answer each one as honestly I could.

"You were trying to be loyal. We could see so clearly what was going on."

My mum's voice was suddenly overshadowed by loud bangs on the door. They left a haunting sound that echoed throughout the kitchen. I froze, realizing that Sam was outside. Ally came running into the kitchen.

"It's him. Quick, get in the toilet. If he comes around the back he won't see us if we're in there."

"Mum, I've got to go, I'll call you in a minute," I whispered.

We both sat staring at each other, huddled in such a small space, waiting for Sam's next move. I was too scared to speak and sat silently praying that he would go away.

Failing to get a response from his knocks, he started to kick the front door. My heart pounded as my mind raced as to what he might try and do. Suddenly he sounded too close for comfort and I realized that he'd pushed open the letterbox and was shouting through it.

"Open the fucking door. I know you're in there, Alice. What the fuck do you think you're doing? Ally, open your fucking front door, I need to speak to my fucking wife."

The shouting got louder and then he pushed his finger on the doorbell and didn't release it. Ally ran upstairs to the children and I knew I had to go to the door.

"Sam, I won't open this door, not whilst you're behaving like this."

"Open the fucking door, Alice, I need to speak to you."

Ally was now standing behind me and I felt stronger knowing that she was there. As I opened the door she hung back, but just enough so that Sam could see her watching him. I opened the door slowly, assuming that he would try and hit me.

"I was worried sick when I got back and you weren't there, Alice. Just get in the car and we can talk when we get home."

He was trying to sound reasonable in front of Ally. I tried to respond calmly in an attempt to diffuse the situation. "I need some time away to think. Please give me some space, Sam."

"Get in the car, Alice. Why do you always do this, why do you always create a drama? Just get in the car."

"No, I'm not coming home with you." It felt so good to say no to him.

"Get in the fucking car now, Alice." Ally moved to my side and stared at him.

"I don't think you heard what Alice said, Sam. She needs some space. She's not coming back with you."

Sam had always been good at keeping his calm around our friends, but it was impossible for him to hold in his temper.

"This is nothing to do with you, Ally, I'm talking to my wife and her place is at home with me. I suggest you fucking stay out of this one."

"Don't you dare talk to me like that," she said as she stepped forward. She had always come across as quite timid, but tonight I was seeing a completely different side to her. "You have no right to talk to me like that."

Sam ignored her, acting as if she wasn't even there. "If this is about you wanting fucking attention, Alice, go and buy that bloody bookcase you keep going on about. Here, take the money and get the fucking thing – is this what this is all about, because I said no to you buying that bloody bookcase?"

"You're mad, do you know that? Do you actually think I'm doing this because of a goddamn bookcase?"

"Just get in the car, Alice, and stop making such a fuss, then we can talk about it."

"I can't talk to you – you don't hear what I say. You never listen to me. It's a waste of time even trying to get you to understand why I'm doing this."

"Shut up, Alice. Get off your high horse and get in the fucking car."

"I'm not getting in the car and I'm not coming home. I've had enough. It's over – I want a divorce."

He grabbed my arm and tried to pull me out of the house. I resisted and held onto the door frame using all the strength I had to stop him dragging me outside.

"Stop it, you're hurting me," I shouted as he pulled on my arm.

"You fucking bitch. It's not enough that you want to humiliate me but now you've brought your friend into this as well. Get in the car."

I was scared but I wasn't going to let him bully me anymore.

"Get off of me."

"No, you're my wife and it's my right to hold you and tell you to come home."

"I'm not coming, go home, Sam. We'll talk in a few days." He glared at me and the look in his eyes told me he was going to get violent. Before I could move away his hand came hard at my face and hit me across the side of my cheek knocking my nose and making my eyes water. Ally screamed.

"I'm going to call the police. They'll do you for domestic violence, you asshole. Get away from my house. I mean it, if you don't leave right now I'm going to call them."

"Don't threaten me, Ally. I'm not leaving until Alice gets in the car."

He had gone too far. Ally walked into the kitchen and called the police. "How dare you hit me, Sam," I said, determined to show him that I would no longer tolerate his behavior towards me. "You better leave now or this is going to get out of hand for you."

"What, go and let you both lie to the police? You've got to be joking, I'm going nowhere. Alice, I need you, don't you dare let me down like this."

"It's always been about you, and never about what I want or need. I will never let you use me again. I've had enough and there's nothing you can say or do to change my mind."

I was finally standing up for myself, and as frightened as I felt standing on that porch begging him to leave, I felt proud of what I was doing.

For an island that took its time with everything, the police turned up very quickly. Literally within ten minutes they were outside the house. Sam tried to play the part of distraught husband, but the police saw right through him. He knew better than to argue with them, and reluctantly got into his car. They gave him a caution and followed him home to ensure he went back there. I was told that if he attempted to come back to Ally's house I could apply for a restraining order.

As I shut the door I ran to the toilet. The first battle had been won but I felt physically sick as a result.

It was over half an hour before I reappeared and Ally sat rubbing my back, trying to reassure me that everything would be ok.

# CHAPTER THIRTEEN

Ally and I were both exhausted and tried to get some rest – but it was impossible for me to shut my eyes, let alone sleep. It was early but I knew Amelia would be up. Not wanting to disturb Ally, I crept downstairs. I was nervous about leaving the house but knew Sam wouldn't be foolish enough to be watching me, and knowing that I could call the police made me feel safer and more in control.

I called my mum back and felt so relieved when she offered to come and be with me and the children. She was a tough cookie and fiercely protective of anything that tried to break the harmony she had tried so hard to create whilst we were growing up. Family was everything to her and it had affected her deeply when I left England to live in St Kitts. It wasn't so much about me moving to another country, but who I was leaving with that mattered most to her.

The journey to Amelia's house took under ten minutes but it felt much longer. I wasn't sure what to expect when I arrived. I drove up and down the road to see if Sam's car was there and felt relieved when I couldn't see it. She looked surprised when I knocked on the door. I deliberately hadn't called her – it was still really early.

"Blimey, you must have been missing the kids badly to have wanted to come and pick them up before breakfast," she joked.

It was obvious by her manner that she knew nothing about the previous night's events and I didn't want to say anything to her.

"I've just got so much to do today, sorry I didn't call but I was on my way..."

"It's no problem," she interrupted.

"Sorry, but I need to get them in the car. I've got to be down town in thirty minutes." I felt awkward about lying to her but I had no choice.

With the kids safely in the car I headed straight back to Ally's house. As we walked through the front door it felt like I was coming home to my safe house – a place where I could think clearly and not be in fear that Sam would just turn up.

I didn't take Archie to school that day. It would have been too easy for Sam to try and take him and I knew instinctively I had to keep the children close to me. Sam had used them as a weapon once before and it was obvious it would now be his first move against me. I told the boys they were having a mini holiday at Ally's which they seemed happy about. When I mentioned that their grandma would be arriving in a few days, Archie's face lit up with excitement. Although he hadn't seen her for a long time they had an amazing bond, and I knew her being around him would soften the blow that we weren't going home.

I knew I had to call my dad. The silence between us had lasted for too long and I knew my mum would have filled him in on all that was going on. I may not have listened to him in regards to Sam, but now I needed his advice more than ever.

I should have known he would be five steps ahead of me, and had already thought about how he could help me. His first suggestion was for me to find a lawyer as quickly as possible. I knew he was right. It would be impossible to reach an amicable agreement with Sam. I had to move quickly, and that meant leaving the safe confines of Ally's house – which I felt uncomfortable about, but had no choice.

I spent the morning trying to find a lawyer and through a series of synchronicities tracked down someone who seemed ideal. Her nickname alone made me feel like I had found the right person. 'The Pit Bull' as she was affectionately known in the industry, was supposedly the best in the business and I was elated when she agreed to meet me that afternoon.

I waited for over an hour before she appeared in the lobby to greet me. Much taller and leaner than I had imagined, she walked purposefully towards me talking as she approached me.

"Sorry I've kept you waiting for so long. The court hearing this morning went over time. I got back as soon I could. Good to meet you. I'm Lucinda. Right, let's get to my office. Follow me."

She reminded me of my junior school headmistress. She had an abrupt manner, and her hair was pulled back tightly in a ponytail. She looked older than I had expected but somehow that made me feel more confident.

For someone who struck me as being so orderly I was surprised when we walked into her office. There were case files everywhere – the floor and every inch of her desk was covered with folders.

"Sorry about the mess. I'm moving my office upstairs so you've caught me right in the middle of sorting everything out."

"It's no problem. You must be busy, are these all live cases?" I said as my eyes wandered around the huge room.

"Yes, every single one of them. I don't really have time to sleep at the moment but it always goes in cycles. In a few months it will be quieter."

"Right. Fire away. Tell me exactly what's happened."

I was so nervous as I started speaking. It felt odd having to open up to a complete stranger, but the more I said the more she seemed to soften towards me, especially when I told her about Sam's violence.

"You need a restraining order in place immediately," she said after she'd let me talk for some time.

"I didn't even know they existed until yesterday. The police mentioned that I could apply for one if Sam went back to my friend's house."

"Right, we need to get one ASAP."

"Can you really do that? Don't I have to wait until he's attacked me? The police made it sound like I could only get one after Sam has actually done something?"

"That's rubbish. I'll get one through in less than twenty-four hours."

I was stunned. Could I really, legally keep him away from me?

"He won't be able to come near you without being arrested. Where are you staying?"

"At my friend's house for the moment. My mum arrives in a few days."

"I want you to move from there. There's a hotel not far from here where I know the manager. He's a very good friend of mine. I want you to go there."

I envied her assertiveness. She was so direct and knew exactly what she wanted to achieve. I watched as she called her friend and booked me a room. It felt good to have someone so strong on my side.

"I'm worried about your safety, I'm not going to lie to you. I've been involved with situations like this before. The man you once knew will be very different now. As soon as he feels he is losing control over you he will try to assert it even more, and I fear it will be through force. I'm not clear yet about your financial situation but I would strongly suggest you have protection whilst you are still on this island."

"Are you suggesting I should have a bodyguard? Once my mum comes out I know I'll feel much safer."

"I have to use my instincts a lot in this profession and I feel very strongly that you need professional protection. Yes, your mother can support you emotionally but not physically. I want you to realize the seriousness of the situation you are in."

Her words had a huge impact on me and I realized how scared I really was.

"I need you to wake up quickly. You are entering into a battle that you have to win for the sake of you and your children's safety. Once you go this route he will view you as his worst enemy."

As I digested what she was saying I felt completely out of

control and couldn't stop crying.

"Good, good...here, have a tissue."

It seemed strange that she was pleased that I was crying. I felt ashamed and weak that I was so tearful.

"This is exactly what I wanted. I need you to be strong and not be in denial about what could possibly go on. You'll feel better soon."

She called her secretary and ordered me a cup of tea with four sugars. I was too upset to say I didn't have sugar, let alone four.

"If you're wondering why I asked for all the sugar – you need it, you're in shock and the sugar will help you."

Psychologically Lucinda had a big effect on me. She forced the self-pity left in me to the surface and made me accept what I had to face. There was no time for wallowing, I had to be strong.

"I need to send someone to court to find out if he's placed an injunction against you. They can check tomorrow morning."

"Sorry to sound stupid but what does an injunction mean?"

"I'm worried he's tried to get an order to stop you from leaving the country. If I was his lawyer it would be the first thing I would advise him to do. It could be up to a year before we could get a court date to overturn the ruling. Don't worry yet, it's just something I need to check for you."

As Lucinda made a phone call I sat in disbelief that Sam could potentially stop me from returning home to England.

I left Lucinda working on securing me a restraining order, and moved from Ally's house into the hotel. Ally came and spent the night with us and in a strange way I enjoyed my first evening there. I knew Sam would be livid that he didn't know where we were but I could only think about the safety of myself and the boys. Once they were sleeping soundly we ordered ourselves room service, and although we were both exhausted managed to drink two bottles of wine.

Ally left in the morning and I drove with the boys to the

airport to collect my mum. Literally at the same time as she landed, Sam was served with a restraining order. I tried not to think about his reaction but it was hard not think about how mad he would be.

Mum was so excited to be with us, and I found her positive attitude infectious. It felt like she had come on a holiday, rather than a mission to see that we got home safely. After we chatted for a few hours I left her to look after the children, and went on my way to visit Lucinda to start compiling my case against Sam.

# CHAPTER FOURTEEN

I was outside the hotel waiting for a taxi when Sam tried his first trick of trying to manipulate me. I knew I was being watched – it was that eerie unexplainable feeling of knowing someone was there. I looked around to see if I could see him. I felt frightened yet powerful, knowing that he couldn't come near me. Instead of Sam I caught sight of Chrissie, an old friend of mine who I hadn't seen for a while. As she walked towards me every instinct in me told me not to trust her.

"Hi, Alice, it's good to see you. I really need to talk to you. Can we talk?" As she spoke she twisted one of her blonde ringlets through her fingers, in that smutty cheerleader type way. She seemed more full of herself than usual and it was obvious that she wanted to talk about Sam.

"Sorry, but I'm really late. I haven't got time. Let's catch up another day."

"Why you are doing this to Sam? He's distraught. All he wants is for you and the kids to come home. You're tearing him apart. Please go home to him. Perhaps you're having some kind of breakdown, but this is no way to behave. What were you thinking with the restraining order? Why have you done this to him?"

I was stunned that she could be so naive and had so readily been taken in by Sam. "I'm not going back to Sam, there's a lot you don't know. If your loyalty's with Sam now then I suggest you stay away from me."

"Alice, I just want to talk to you, that's all."

The taxi pulled up and I stepped forward to get in.

"Can I ride with you?"

"No, it's not a good idea."

"Oh, my God, what's happened to us being friends?"

"You've obviously decided to take Sam's side. Please leave me alone." I was surprised by how cold I sounded, but I was upset that she had got involved and was only seeing things from Sam's perspective.

"I'm doing this for you, Alice. I can't see you tear the family apart."

Just before I got into the taxi she showed me her spiteful side that I always knew lingered within her. "He won't let you get away with this, you could destroy his whole reputation if you carry on like this. What the hell do you think you're doing?"

I ignored her and got into the taxi and shut the door as quickly as I could.

"You alright, ma'am," the taxi driver asked, as he tried to sum me up through his rearview mirror.

"I think so." I wasn't in the mood to talk as I played back everything Chrissie had said to me. Sam's reputation was at stake and I knew he would fight to stop me from tarnishing the cool image he had worked so hard to create, but getting her on side was a pathetic attempt to try and win me over.

"How yo enjoying ta island, ma'am? You been ta the fesh market yet? My cousin, he run the most famous hut in town ya know. I can give ya his name if you wanna go?"

"I haven't had time," I replied, trying to be polite but short.

"Oh, ma'am, yo can't leave without goin to ta fesh market."

"I'll try but there's lots I still need to do," I said pretending to be a tourist. There was something so relaxing about imagining I was on the island having a wonderful time.

"Yo make sure ta check out my cousin, he a good man, ma'am. He go by the name of Famous Joe – you won't be missin his sign."

"Thank you," I said as I handed over my money. "It was good talking to you, I'll make sure I pay him a visit before I leave." He had offered me a few moments of light relief without even knowing it.

As I walked into Lucinda's reception I was brought back to reality very quickly. I sat waiting for her, biting what was left of my nails. Her assistant appeared and I followed her into Lucinda's office.

"He's applied for an injunction, this changes everything," she said as soon as I walked through the door. She was so matter-of-fact in the way she spoke. "I was hoping he hadn't done it because this makes everything so much more confrontational, but you don't really have a choice now."

"What does that actually mean?" I asked, feeling completely out of control and panicked by what she had just said.

"The worst-case scenario is that you can't leave the country until we can get a court date. Don't worry, there's always a way around everything, I just have to start thinking fast."

My heart sank as she explained what it meant to me.

"It's not as bad as it seems. We'll just have to take a different stance now. You can't stay here until we get a court date. We'll try to negotiate first through his lawyer. If that fails, somehow we'll get you out of here. I'm toying with the idea of suggesting that he withdraws the injunction at the same time as we withdraw the restraining order, and then he allows you to go back to England immediately after that. In exchange for you going to England perhaps you could agree to him keeping most of the possessions? I want you to serve him with divorce papers the moment you reach England, I don't want to start anything here. I just need to check your status. Are you a resident here?"

"Yes, we all are."

"But you and the children are still British citizens? Would you be happy to invoke your residency here?"

"Yes, of course. I'll do anything to get back to England and away from him."

"My plan is to get you out of here and then I have a lawyer in London that you can go to straight away to start the divorce proceedings."

"Don't I have to file for a divorce here? I thought because we all live here..."

"No, the fact that you are all British citizens means you have a right to file for divorce in the UK. You can't do it here. He's too manipulative and knows too many people, and the fact that he's got this injunction means he doesn't want you to leave. He's a big fish in a small pond but he must believe he can still control you. The moment you leave, everything changes for him, which is why I don't hold out much hope of being able to negotiate with him. I'm coming around to the idea that you might have to leave illegally."

"How can I leave if there's an injunction on me?"

"Where there's a will there's a way. I need to think about it."

I went outside for a cigarette and left Lucinda chewing over what felt like some very limited options for me. The anxiety I felt was overwhelming. She had delivered the news in a calm way but I knew the seriousness of what she had said. Sam had put an injunction on me to stop me from leaving the country. It was my worst nightmare coming true, yet Lucinda didn't seem too phased by the news. I had faith in her but couldn't help feeling that Sam was completely in control. I lit another cigarette. I wasn't ready to go back in.

"I wondered where you'd disappeared to, are you ok?"

"Sorry, I just needed to get some fresh air."

"I think I've got a plan, but I need to phone London first and check a few things."

She didn't elaborate on her idea but mentioned it could involve me having to leave the island sooner than I had thought.

Back at the hotel I explained everything to my mum. She sat speechless and then asked lots of questions that I couldn't answer. She wanted to know how quickly the injunction could become effective but I didn't know. To her it was the most obvious question I could have asked, but I wasn't thinking clearly when I was in Lucinda's office.

"Can't we just leave before the airport is notified? I thought everything took ages here?"

Her eyes were pleading with me to give her the answer that she wanted to hear, but I felt like my fate lay in the hands of Lucinda and I wasn't clear about what her plan actually involved. I knew I couldn't just make a decision to leave, however tempting it was to just jump on the next plane back to the UK. The more we talked, the more trapped I felt, but I tried to remain positive believing that there would be a solution. As we sat talking in the hotel restaurant I spotted one of Sam's work colleagues at a table in the corner of the room.

"Don't look now, but someone who Sam works with is sitting just to the right of the bar."

"Swap places with me so he can't see you," my mum said in a strong, protective way.

I lowered my head and moved into her chair. I felt uncomfortable knowing that he was there and we quickly finished eating. We tried to get up discreetly. As we reached the door he came over to us.

"This must be Mum," he said with a sarcastic smile. I said hello and carried on walking.

"I've got a message from Sam that he wants me to give you. He would have preferred to bring it himself but I understand he can't. He asked me to read you this note, it will only take a minute."

"I don't want to hear it."

"Don't be like that, Alice. It's only short."

"Please leave me alone." I walked away from him, and Mum followed a few steps behind me. He knew I was serious and decided not to follow.

"I'm so proud of the way you just reacted," she said as we waited for the lift. "The Alice of old would never have stood up for herself like that."

As she gave me a hug she had no idea how good she had made me feel. I needed her love more than ever.

I was tearful at breakfast the following morning, thinking about the worst that could happen. I felt sunken that I might have to stay and say goodbye to my mum and face living on the island alone with the children. The hope that I had felt in the previous few days was starting to wane and I wasn't sure I had the strength to keep fighting Sam. Yes, the physical violence could no longer hurt me, but the mental torture was almost unbearable.

# CHAPTER FIFTEEN

The following two days were hard to get through and I felt more trapped than ever. I was at the hands of my lawyer and nothing she said made me feel secure. Her plan was for us to leave before the injunction came into full effect, but although she said it was my best option, she had many reservations about the idea and wanted to be one hundred percent sure before she gave her instructions. I felt cheated by the legal system. How could Sam have been granted an injunction to enforce me to stay in a country I had no support in, at the mercy of a man who clearly wanted revenge?

As I made my way to my next meeting with Lucinda I hoped that I would walk away feeling either relief or more upbeat about my situation. I kissed the kids goodbye and watched as they playfully jumped in and out of the swimming pool, oblivious to the fate that lay ahead of them. They looked so happy and I knew I was doing the right thing for them in the long run too. I had no doubt that through watching the way their father behaved towards me, they would have followed by his example, and that scared me more than anything. Their beautiful innocence corrupted by the savage impulses of a man they looked up to and admired. Yes, it would be hard for them in the short term, but I knew they would benefit from not being around Sam all the time.

I was shocked when Lucinda greeted me with a beaming smile, and immediately felt excited.

"I have some great news. Let's get into my office first and then I'll tell you."

I couldn't walk up the stairs quick enough. It was as if the pounding beats of my heart were urging me upwards as fast as possible to hear what Lucinda had to say.

"The injunction won't go into effect for another two days," she said before I'd even had time to shut the door. "It's great news – all we need to do now is plan how to get you off the island without Sam knowing. It's the only way."

How could she make me feel ecstatic in one breath, and then totally fearful in another?

"How can I leave without him knowing? He knows all the staff at the airport, I just don't know how I could get away without him finding out?"

"We're going to get you out of here, Alice. I need your help now."

As she stood up and walked purposefully over to the window she gestured with her hands as if she was writing in the air. I imagined her in front of a blackboard carefully building her game plan bit by bit, as she scribbled away in earnest.

"Think, Alice, I need you to think. I know you've got it in you to run, you've got the support of your mother, and what means more to you – your freedom, or being trapped here for possibly up to two years? That's what it could be you know? It could take two years to get the injunction lifted and legally get you back to Britain."

"Two years?" I was horrified that it could take so long.

"He thinks he's been clever. He knows how slow everything is here, but if we get you to England, the ball will be back in your court – although you do stand the chance of him filing child-abduction charges against you. That's what I've been working with our office in London on."

"Oh God, what does that mean?" I felt like someone had kicked me in the stomach as I felt my balance go and held onto the arm of the chair for fear I was going to fall over.

"Alice, are you ok?"

"He's got me, hasn't he?" I said, feeling faint. Everything seemed to go hazy as I literally fell into the chair. "I don't really have a way out, do I? If I run he'll get me anyway and if I stay..."

"Please, Alice, I need you to focus and stay positive. Even if he were to file abduction charges you would be able to fight to get them overturned."

"But where's the justice?"

"Alice, you've got to stay positive. We're going to get you out of this situation but you need to stay strong to make it happen."

The reality of what I had to do started to sink in. It was illegal for me to run with the children without Sam's permission, but he would never give it anyway. It really was my only option, but I knew he would do everything he could to stop me or make us come back.

"Alice, I need you to make a decision quickly. These are your only choices – to stay here for up to two years or to leave and perhaps face the consequences of a court hearing against you – but you'll be in England, you'll have a strong case and you'll be benefiting from the support of your family."

# CHAPTER SIXTEEN

My mind was made up. The following day I was going to run. I would accept graciously that I could take virtually no belongings with me – my freedom meant more than anything material I had ever owned. Nothing was more important now than getting away from Sam.

We decided against the airport as my route out of the country. It was too risky – we would leave by boat instead. The journey would be a long one, and once we reached Antigua we would board a plane direct to London. I was content that I was making the right move for myself and the children. I knew Sam would be shocked and want revenge on me but there was no way I could reason with him to legally allow us to leave the country. In an ironic twist of fate he had forced me to flee the country without him knowing.

Whilst Lucinda's assistant booked our boat and plane tickets I rushed back to the hotel to explain the plan to my mum. She was shocked that we had to leave so quickly, but ecstatic that we were actually going.

We decided to make the journey into an adventure for the kids and told them how exciting it was going to be. They bought into our enthusiasm and I went off to buy sweets and toys to keep them entertained for the long journey ahead of us back to the UK.

I made my way to the other side of the island knowing I wouldn't bump into any of Sam's friends – but I still spent the entire time looking over my shoulder. Whilst I was deciding what to buy I thought about Nathan and how special our time together had been. I owed so much to him for helping me to gain the strength to leave Sam and knew I had to see him before I left. I called him in the hope of meeting up in the afternoon.

"Can I pop by and see you later? I've got to leave the island but I really want to see you before I go."

"You're leaving?"

"Sam's put an injunction on me and if I don't go now I'll be trapped here and life will be..."

"You must be under so much pressure, I totally understand. When do you go?"

"Tomorrow."

"Come over to the house, I'll be there from 5:00 onwards."

I felt sad when Nathan answered the door, knowing how much I would miss him, but I tried to put on a brave face as he greeted me. We sat outside and drank tea. I wanted a glass of wine but he was so excited by his latest herbal find that I didn't want to offend him by asking for anything else.

The conversation flowed from one thing to another, but we spoke mostly about me leaving the island. We reminisced about how we had become friends and I thanked him for how much he had helped me. It was in that moment, as I looked at him and said thank you that I knew there was more to say. I knew if I didn't say something I would regret it for the rest of my life.

"I have feelings for you," I blurted out before I'd properly thought about the consequences. "I think I'm in love with you," I said, unsure if it was really true deep down or based on the unconditional help he had offered me in helping me to leave Sam.

I don't really know what I was expecting him to say. I looked away and stared down at the floor whilst I felt his eyes on me. I heard him move uncomfortably in his chair as if he was frantically searching for something to say, not knowing how to answer me. The silence was excruciating and I felt myself sweating from the pressure of the situation.

I'm not sure how long we were sat like that, but as every second went by it became more awkward – my eyes down on the floor and him watching me – neither of us having the courage to speak. Then, taking me completely by surprise, he leaned forward and took hold of my hand.

"I care so much about you as a friend, Alice. I hope we can keep in touch. I'd like to hear about how you get on in England."

I'm not sure what made me feel worse – being rejected by Nathan or the embarrassment of what I had said to him.

"Perhaps it's best I go?"

"Ok, if you feel that's best. It's been great to see you."

We hugged as if we'd only known each other a short while, he wished me luck and I went on my way feeling sunken that our friendship had ended so abruptly and that I would probably never see him again. I knew in my heart that I had just ruined one of the most beautiful relationships I had ever experienced.

# THE RISE OF ISIS

# CHAPTER SEVENTEEN

After a long and tiring journey back to British soil we finally arrived safely into the confines of Gatwick airport. Never before had it felt so good to see the grey clouds of Great Britain. We had made it. I knew there would be huge repercussions, but I felt stronger knowing I was back where I belonged.

It was great to see my dad and sister waiting for us at the airport. I couldn't hold back as we embraced one another after over a year of being apart – I shook as I cried. An overwhelming feeling of relief washed over me – I was back on British soil and it felt fantastic.

Amidst the joy of the family reunion, I feared that Sam was planning his revenge. As suggested by my lawyer, I sent him an email telling him that the children and I were in England, staying at my parents' house. I made it clear that I needed to be back with my family and offered him access if he wanted to come to England to see the boys – but stated my case clearly as to why I wasn't ready to return to the Bahamas with them.

I felt unnerved that I hadn't heard back from him and paranoia set in every time I left my parents' house.

It was a week later when he eventually called. I was caught off-guard as I answered the phone and froze when I heard his voice.

"You've made the biggest mistake of your fucking life. I'll get you for this and make your life living hell. If you don't come back to me, you just watch what I'll do to you. I'm giving you your last chance to get back to where you belong, but if you don't, expect life to take some nasty turns for you."

I slammed the phone down and stood with my back against the wall, shaking. Part of me was so frightened of what he might try and do, yet there was also a side that felt so much relief that

I had got away from him.

Within twenty-four hours I had been granted a restraining order that was effective in the UK. I felt safer knowing Sam couldn't just turn up at the house, but worried that he would be watching me. I kept wondering to what extent he'd go to seek his revenge on me and knew I couldn't let the children out of my sight.

A week went by without hearing another word from him. He had been served with the divorce papers, but still nothing. I started to suffer from severe panic attacks being unable to control the fear that was building by the day. Although I was reassured that if he tried to harm me he would put his whole future at risk, I was still frightened of what he might do – even with the restraining order in place. Waking up and admitting to myself I was in an abusive relationship had forced me to confront many issues – one of which was the reality that I had married a man without a conscience. It was the understanding of what that really meant that frightened me more than anything else.

I was the only one in the house when the doorbell rang. I peered out of the upstairs window and saw two policemen standing on the doorstep. The image of their uniformed silhouettes made me nervous but I was convinced their visit was in relation to the restraining order. Before I'd fully opened the door the taller of the two started speaking.

"Are you Alice Bailey?"

"Yes."

"You have been charged under the Hague Convention Act with Child Abduction. You will be summoned within the next seven days to appear at the High Court of Justice, and due to the charge that has been brought against you, we need you to surrender your passport. Please confirm that Archie James Bailey is your son and resides with you, and also that George Jay Bailey is your son and resides with you. We need to take their passports too."

It was one of those moments normally witnessed in an epic film – the emotional climax of the main character being brought to their knees by something happening outside of themselves. I stared blankly at the policemen and felt a haze surround me, disabling me from seeing anything clearly. Everything fell silent. A peaceful sense of floating ensued, interrupted by a loud voice coming from inside my head: *"You're a criminal. You're going to be tried for child abduction. You're a criminal. You're a criminal."* The voice got louder and louder until it forced my body to the floor. An arm tried to catch my fall, helping me cushion the impact of collapsing onto the ground.

"Are you ok?"

"I'm not sure," I said, unable to move.

"You're in shock. Just sit still for a few minutes."

I felt like a robot following instructions without the ability to think about what I was doing. I stood up, walked into the house and found our passports. I handed them over to the police, and then signed three forms, not really reading what they were, or understanding clearly why I had to sign them. I should have asked lots of questions but I was unable to.

I closed the door and sank against the back of it. I felt paralyzed. I tried to move, but it was impossible to get up. Any hope I had had of a life away from Sam had been shattered. I knew he would ensure that he won the court case and I would be forced back to St Kitts. I felt so foolish – I had got caught up in wanting to get away from Sam at any cost, but now the consequences were crippling and I was more out of control than ever before.

I was surprised by how calmly my dad reacted to the news when he arrived home that evening. He had been expecting it and had already discussed my options with the UK lawyer, who believed I had a strong enough case to overturn the charge.

The following morning I was in the lawyer's office starting the drawn-out process of defending myself. I sat for hours talking into a tape recorder reliving some terrifying moments from my past, whilst my lawyer and her assistant sat whispering to one another. It felt uncomfortable having to open up in front of them, but I had no choice and tried to pretend that they weren't there.

"Did he ever try to actually kill you?" she asked me as I stopped talking to take a sip of water. I answered as emotionless as the question had been asked.

"He threatened to, but never actually did."

"That rules out one defense straight away. Ok, carry on, we need you to be as factual as possible. Try to focus on dates, times and witnesses as you're talking. Witnesses are the key if we're going to run with *grave risk.*"

I carried on speaking, not really understanding what she had said. Three cups of coffee later and realizing I was suffering from severe exhaustion they decided to call it a night. We had five days to file an affidavit, with the seventh being my appearance in court.

The next day my lawyer phoned after listening to my hours of outpouring.

"Right, we're going to run with *grave risk*. We've got to prove that returning the children to St Kitts will expose them to psychological harm. It's not going to be an open and shut case. We've got to try and prove that the abuse you've been suffering from has and will have severe psychological effects on the children. Are you prepared for Archie to be interviewed by an appointed counsellor? Have you had counselling yourself? Can you get me your files as soon as possible? Who did you see? Are they legitimate? I need details today."

I didn't want the children to be involved, but I knew what Archie had witnessed and thought it might be helpful if he talked to a professional about what he had seen and heard. I wasn't sure if he would tell the truth but I didn't feel I had a choice. The best outcome would be that he benefitted from the counselling – the worst that it brought up memories that he had tried hard to forget and would refuse to talk about them.

A few days later I learnt the reality of what the counsellor had uncovered from his time with Archie. I had spent so long trying to deny the seriousness of my situation with Sam that I never once stopped to consider the awful impact it was having on Archie. They say that some of the greatest truths come from a child's mouth and Archie's perspective on all that had gone on was astounding. He had also remembered events that I had forgotten to mention. Most upsetting was his obvious fear of his father. I cried and cried as I read the transcript – the innocent voice of a child traumatized by the very environment that was supposed to nurture him.

There was some relief alongside the shock of understanding what Archie had endured. He agreed to continue with the counselling sessions and I knew from my own experience that it would help to clear the burden that I felt responsible for putting on him.

The next day my affidavit was sent off to Sam's lawyer, but Archie's statements were held back. A trick of the trade I came to understand. They would be included at the last minute to avoid any attempt for him to be manipulated.

# CHAPTER EIGHTEEN

Day seven arrived, and with it I found myself shaking outside The High Court of Justice. I sat waiting for the barrister to arrive. It was a strange feeling knowing my fate lay in the hands of a man I had met for less than an hour the previous evening. I watched Sam turn up, ensuring that he couldn't see me. He looked so smug laughing and joking with his legal team – so confident that justice would reign on his side. I was determined to avoid any eye contact with him and felt sick that we would be sitting so closely in the courtroom. I wondered if the judge would see through all his lies, and knew if I lost the case I would be sent back to St Kitts within days of the conclusion of the hearing. My overriding fear was that I was up against an enemy that would stop at nothing to win the battle I had effectively started, but I had been his victim long before I had reacted against him.

"Court rise." I stood up to signal the arrival of the judge. Our respective barristers took their turn to speak, as they both outlined their arguments. I sat trying to listen to everything that was being said, but it was hard to follow. As the toing and froing became more intense there was frantic whispering from our opposition. It became evident that they were trying to throw Archie's statements out of court. As both barristers approached the judge I prayed that he would allow the statements to be included.

To my relief their plea was denied, and we enjoyed our first small victory – but it felt insignificant in comparison to the bigger battle that we had to win. As I subtly looked across at Sam and his team I saw them huddled and sensed the intensity of what they were talking about. I wondered if they had a trick up their sleeve. My barrister had urged me to stay strong, so I tried to remain positive that the outcome of the day would be one we would come to celebrate.

Sat in front of me was the man who would speak on Archie's behalf. As he was called to the front of the courtroom I felt apprehensive about what he would say. I wondered how Sam would react to his findings. As I sat listening to the heart-wrenching honesty of an eight-year-old, I wondered if Archie's statements stirred any remorse within Sam – but I held back from looking at him.

The court was called into recess for an hour's lunch break after which we would return for the final statements and ruling. As I walked out of the courtroom I could feel Sam staring at me. Maybe he believed that I had manipulated Archie into saying the things he had, but either way I knew it must have come as a shock to him.

Lunch turned into the longest hour I had ever experienced. Unsure of the judge's decision, I was too nervous to eat. I sat playing with my food praying that he would see through Sam's lies and believe what Archie had said. I kept looking at my watch, knowing that each minute was taking me closer to the ruling that would affect my future for the better or worse. I was hanging in the middle of a life made of heaven or hell, and knew the scales could tip either way. Even a reassuring word from my barrister did little to convince me that I would be able to stay in England.

Every cell in my body was on edge as I waited for the fate of my future to be read out in the courtroom. The judge stared straight at me and addressed me directly.

"Young lady, by all accounts for leaving the way you did you should be sent back to where you have illegally come from. But I have made my decision, and whilst I am not in the business of tearing families apart, on this occasion feel that it is in the interest of your children's psychological health to remain in England. I hereby confirm that there is, without doubt, grave risk to the children if they return to the family home in St Kitts. I order that the children be named habitually resident in the United Kingdom and that a monthly maintenance payment be agreed by the plaintiff, and seen by myself before this court is adjourned."

As I realized what the judge had decided I wanted to run up and kiss him. Justice had been served and I felt euphoric that I had a legal seal of approval to stay in the UK. The air around us suddenly felt so much lighter and tears of joy streamed down my face as the news sunk in. I didn't turn to look at Sam as I walked out of the room. I tried to act dignified, not wanting to rub salt into the newly opened wound that would be festering within him.

Once we were outside I ran up to the barrister and gave him a hug. He was a stranger, yet someone I would forever remember as having had such a positive impact on my life. I knew I was just another number to him – a case file that could now be closed – but he would always be special to me. I was in awe at the way he had delivered my defense – his humble, yet authoritative manner was like something out of a courtroom drama and I walked away knowing I would never forget him.

We celebrated that evening into the early hours of the morning. The sweet taste of success lingered on my lips as I enjoyed glass after glass of champagne with my family. After years of heartache I felt like I was finally on my way to enjoying life again. Of course, the divorce was still to come, and I was aware of how difficult that would be, but something in me knew it would seem a breeze compared to what I had just been through. If life was a comparison of experiences, I knew the one I had just left behind would be my pedestal of painful encounters.

I made a vow to myself that night that Sam would no longer get the better of me. I had been granted my ticket to freedom and I was going to make the most of it.

# CHAPTER NINETEEN

It took me a while to find my feet, and although I suffered from bad days, each new day brought me closer to loving life again. I often wondered what Sam was up to. It had been three months since the court case and we hadn't heard a word from him. As confusing as it was for the children, there was a sense of relief that life was now calm.

I decided to overcome my pride and email Nathan to fill him in on everything that had happened since I left St Kitts. I was careful to make sure I sounded friendly, but not too familiar and felt awkward as I clicked send. He replied quickly but I knew from his formal tone that our friendship was better off being left to the memories in St Kitts – there was nothing I could do to force the friendship to continue. Perhaps we had both needed each other at the time, and now we had moved on in our separate ways. I felt comforted by the belief that some friendships were meant to last a lifetime, whilst others came and went at key moments, perhaps playing the part of pushing you forward, helping you to fulfill your destiny.

It didn't take long for the children to settle into their new school. I watched with admiration as they made new friends and adapted quickly to the environment around them. Knowing that they were happy gave me the confidence to focus on finding a job. Although my background was in journalism it had been over ten years since I'd written for a newspaper or magazine and I knew I wouldn't be able to go straight back into it. Not really being sure what I could do, I applied for various local jobs as a stepping stone to eventually getting back into a job that involved writing.

A short stint at the local bookshop gave me too much time to think, and I worried that I would never be able to get back into writing again, yet I enjoyed the relaxation of being in a quiet environment and found the job to be really therapeutic. Every now and again a little voice from within would question why I wasn't returning to journalism and I started to think that maybe I should.

After a month of being at the bookshop I was flicking through the local paper when I noticed a recruitment advert for a staff reporter. I called to find out more information, and after an informal chat agreed to send in my CV.

I was nervous when I got a reply a few days later. I opened the envelope slowly, expecting it to be a letter of rejection, but was surprised to read that they wanted me to submit some examples of my work and style. In the rush to leave St Kitts I had left behind all my magazine and newspaper cuttings. Whilst I hadn't enjoyed many bylines, the ones that I had achieved were proudly pasted into a scrap book that I assumed would now be reduced to ash. As an alternative to showing them copy I had actually had published I spent a few days making up sample stories, trying to follow their house style. I sent them off and waited for their response. I heard back a week later and was asked to go for an interview. Two days after that I was offered the job, and agreed to start the following month. The whole process was so painless that it didn't feel real. I felt excited that I was entering back into the world I had been so comfortable in before leaving for St Kitts, and that it had happened so seamlessly.

It was a great team to work alongside and it wasn't long before I felt like a firm fixture of the paper. I was involved in everything from reporting, to sub-editing and I relished in the fact that no two days were ever the same.

A few months later I was moved to the features desk and I enjoyed being able to get stuck into an issue, rather than just reporting the news. It wasn't long before I was included in features meetings and took pride in being able to give feedback and suggest ideas for upcoming articles.

In one particular meeting the editor expressed her concern that the paper lacked a personal touch. She wanted ideas about including an advice page where the paper could interact directly with its readers, offering them answers to some of their problems.

"What kind of advice are you thinking about?" I asked, knowing exactly what I wanted to suggest.

"General advice – although ideally I'd like to focus on financial advice – I want to steer away from relationship issues as we could end up out of our depth."

"We could try and get a local financial advisor on board to answer reader's problems," I suggested, really wishing it could be an agony aunt.

"I like that idea, Alice. Perhaps you could write a column that focuses on a different financial aspect each week. It could be basic things like how to be economical with your weekly shop or the escalating costs of entertaining the children. I feel that would encourage readers to write in at first."

I agreed, even though I had no financial experience whatsoever, and the following month we added our new letters pages into the newspaper, alongside my column which I struggled to write.

A few months later I was promoted to Deputy Features Editor, and it felt great to be doing something I really enjoyed. As my confidence grew at work I started to feel more sociable and made an effort to get back in touch with old friends. I was surprised by how many people had moved back to the area, and some had stayed in contact with one another.

With little effort I was warmly welcomed back into a circle of friends I had literally left behind when I moved to St Kitts. There was a familiarity and closeness when we got together that I had never felt with anyone I had met during my time away, and I made it a priority to meet with them once a week. To start with it was on a Saturday for lunch but soon we pushed one another to go out in the evening without the children, where we could relax and have some fun. It seemed to be what everyone needed, some time out away from the drudgery of trying to balance too many things.

Our nights out were genuinely about a group of friends enjoying good company. At first we kept our outings to local restaurants and bars but we soon tired of the same scenery and ventured further afield into the city. We saw our weekly jaunts as an opportunity to let our hair down and have fun together, and were mostly hostile to any man that tried to invade our space – with the exception of Sonia, who openly welcomed them to join us. She was a seductress in every sense of the word and made it her mission not to buy herself one drink when we were out. On most occasions she walked away from her pursuer, but there had been times when the lure of uncharted water became too much for her to resist. We all had an unspoken agreement that we would never mention what had gone on – after all, we often saw her leave but knew nothing about what happened after that. She never spoke about what she did when she left us behind in a bar, and none of us ever asked. We didn't judge, knowing what a terrible time she was having at home. In a strange way we hoped it would give her the confidence to get out of the situation she was in.

Sonia and I often spoke about the parallels we shared in our lives and I understood how difficult it was for her to just leave without having somewhere safe to go to. She didn't have the support that I had been offered by my family and that made it even harder for her to find the strength to take any action. As the weeks went by she became more desperate to try and find someone who could take care of her, but from what we assumed she had only found people who wanted to use her for sex. We watched sadly as her self-esteem plummeted and prayed that she'd get the courage to go at it alone. Then one night she seemed so much happier, and that's when we found out about Ronnie.

"I know you all think I'm a slut but you know deep down there's more to me than that. I need to get something off my chest and want some advice," she said nervously as she sunk her teeth into her bottom lip.

We all sat listening, not saying a word. Yes, she had been out of control in the way she sometimes behaved but how she thought we viewed her wasn't true. We were concerned for her more than anything else and wanted her to be happy.

"Do you remember the guy that I met when we were in the I-Bar?" We nodded and she carried on. "Well I've been seeing him ever since and I really think we've got an amazing connection. There's something different about him and he really seems to like me. He always wants to hold my hand and I love it."

"Go on, tell us the truth – are you having great sex with him?" Chloe interrupted.

"No, and that's one of the things I love most about him. He hasn't tried to get me in bed. We spend ages cuddling and he's always touching me, just not under my clothes yet, if you know what I mean?"

"Has he not even tried to kiss you?" Amy asked.

"No, he kisses me on the cheek but we haven't kissed properly yet."

"What? Don't you get the urge to want to?"

"Yeah, course I do, I really fancy him, but every time we're together we just talk or cuddle up and watch a film or TV and we haven't gone past that yet."

"Aren't you frustrated?"

"Yes, but it just hasn't happened yet and I suppose I'm just really enjoying the time we spend together. That's what makes it so different."

"Can't you initiate something? Maybe he's really shy?"

"God no. What if I did and he pulled away? Maybe he's just the type of person who likes to take things really slowly. Look where rushing into something got me with Dave?

"Maybe he's gay?" Sarah piped up from across the table. "You never know these days?"

"Shut up, Sarah, he's not gay," Sonia replied defensively.

"Aren't you just a tiny bit suspicious?" she pushed.

"No, I'm not, but I'm starting to regret talking to you about him."

"Oh come on, I'm only having some fun with you. It's a bit unusual you've got to admit that?"

Being the natural diplomat, Gemma tried to bring the conversation back to the level Sonia felt comfortable with. "You're right, babes, taking it at his pace is probably better, and then when the passion does come…"

"I'll explode. Imagine if it goes on like this for another few weeks? Actually, I might think he's gay if that happens."

"When we were at school and I fancied someone that wasn't interested in me, my mum always said, 'They must be gay, darling'," said Sarah trying to bridge the gap between her and Sonia.

"Did you leave school thinking our entire class was gay?" Sonia couldn't resist the banter.

"Ha bloody ha."

"Oh come on, don't be so bloody sensitive, you always had a boyfriend. Do you know I was jealous of you for years? You seemed to have a boyfriend from when we first started school and I really wanted one too but it never happened for me until we were in the sixth form."

"Shut up, you weren't jealous of me? Look at the awful boyfriends I always had. You did have a boyfriend when we were in the fifth year."

"No, I didn't."

"You did, don't you remember 'Johnny Long socks?'"

"Oh my God, 'Johnny Long Socks', I can't believe you remembered his nickname."

"Who the hell was 'Johnny Long Socks'?" I asked. I was in the same class but didn't remember him.

"He was the really tall one who always had his socks pulled up just below his knees."

"Did we actually call him that to his face?"

"Yeah, course we did."

"He probably loved his long socks and thought he was really cool."

"Think we put a stop to that. He didn't have the worst nickname. You must remember 'Miranda Melons'?"

"That wasn't her real name was it?"

"No, don't you remember how big her boobs were?"

"Tell me she didn't know we called her that?"

"Oh yes she did."

"What is it about labeling people with their most embarrassing attribute? I bet to this day she's trying to make them smaller. She's probably had a breast reduction because of us."

"Anyway, enough about them, I need some advice. Ronnie's asked me to go away with him for a week. I so want to go but what shall I tell Dave? What I really want to know is if anyone will cover for me so that I can say I'm away with you?"

It seemed that I was the obvious choice because I didn't know Dave, so he wouldn't think to call me. Also, I didn't have a husband that Dave could come into contact with.

"All right," I said. "Use me. Where're we going, anywhere nice?"

"I love you, Alice, thank you so much." She gave me a big hug and we agreed to talk about the finer details nearer the time.

# CHAPTER TWENTY

Our girl's nights out took on a life of their own and within six months there were about ten of us who committed once a week to uninhibited 'me time'. We'd built up a strong bond and I always looked forward to our weekly gatherings. The night would always start by politely asking each other how we were and then after a few glasses of wine the truth would come out. Everyone was miserable in one way or another. Financial pressure alone was starting to take its toll as the recession closed in on us.

I felt much freer than most of my friends, in that I didn't have a husband telling me what I could and couldn't spend. Virtually everyone was rebelling by being on our girl's night outs – which were viewed by most of their partners as unnecessary jaunts that didn't have a place in their recession-proof plans.

A single friend wanted to join us and I worried slightly about the dynamics, which is why I had delayed asking her to come along. Katy always said what she thought – often without thinking. She had offended me many times but I had come to love the fact that I could always rely on her to give me an honest, straight opinion. For others she was too much, and as a result had alienated a lot of people. She was going through an anti-men stage of life and I prayed that she would just enjoy a fun night out rather than engage anyone in her usual opinionated arguments. I called and asked her to join us the following evening, and she was excited to finally be invited along.

The night Katy came out with us was a special celebration. I had been promoted at work and Sonia was celebrating her birthday. We decided to be decadent and ordered champagne. Whenever we all got really drunk together sex always seemed to be our hot topic of conversation and after weaving around various subjects we found ourselves back at our favorite one.

"I've been married for nine years but if I'm being honest, sex has always been boring between us. God, if any of you ever repeat that I'll kill you," said Jenny.

"I so know what you mean. I can't help thinking half the time that Philip's getting off a lot more than I am," Stacey said.

"I get more turned on when I'm by myself," said Sarah.

Everyone stared at her, waiting for her to say more.

"Oh come on. Don't all look so surprised? Who doesn't enjoy being by themselves? I know exactly what I like and can hit the spot without the fumbling."

"It's one of the reasons why I don't want a man in my life at the moment," piped up Katy. "I've perfected the art of self-pleasure to the point where I don't need anyone else."

"If that's true then you should be an amazing lover," I teased. "Isn't half the battle behind having a great sex life knowing what turns you on?"

"Get you Miss Sex Therapist."

"I'm serious. If you know what you like and can communicate it then that must lead to satisfaction rather than frustration."

"I never tell Jason what to do," said Amber. "I just let him get on with it. He never really turns me on anymore – not sure if he really ever did?"

"I bet you don't know what you like?" Katy said.

"Perhaps I don't, but if I did I don't think I'd say it to him anyway."

"You wouldn't ever say if you liked something he was doing, or tell him what you wanted?"

"No, I wouldn't. I'm really shy about stuff like that."

"I give Jim signs if I like something," said Chloe. "But I'd never tell him what to do in bed. He always leads and I love it that way."

"We hardly ever do it anymore," said Gemma. "But that's normal isn't it, after three kids and 13 years of marriage? Most of the time I can't be bothered."

"I agree," said Beau. "I think sex is overrated anyway. I just haven't got the energy – I'm always too tired to think about it, let alone actually do it."

We were all huddled around one table with our chairs pushed closely together. The bar was noisy but none of us really cared who could be listening.

"There's always time for a bit of self-pleasure," said Katy. "Come on, girls, what are we all doing? It's so relaxing. I don't think anything can beat the feeling of an orgasm."

"I don't know where you get the time?" Jenny said. "The last thing I could think about before I went to bed was making myself come – even if Simon wasn't next to me."

"Yes, you would if you knew what you were missing out on. It's just about making the time to indulge yourself. What's the big deal anyway it doesn't have to take long?"

"How can you be so self-assured?" Jenny said, getting annoyed by where the conversation was going.

"Once you try it you'll know what I mean. Why would you feel guilty about it? Get over the belief that we've just been given our private parts to make kids and serve our other halves."

"I don't think that."

"Then why are you getting so defensive with me?"

"I've never served Simon, as you so horribly put it. Look it's really simple – I don't have the inclination or time to play with myself." Jenny was now trying to be as condescending to Katy as she had been with her, but it went straight over Katy's head.

"When was the last time you had sex?"

"About six weeks ago. You must be so shocked by that?"

"You must be so frustrated?"

"No, I'm not. It's just part of life."

"Don't you worry that he's gone elsewhere?"

"Hey," I jumped in. "That's out of order, shut up, Katy." I was regretting ever inviting her along. I felt stupid for even thinking that she could have got through the night without insulting someone.

"How dare you insinuate that Simon might be having an affair," Jenny said.

"Who do you think you are?" said Gemma glaring at Katy.

"I don't have to listen to this crap," Jenny said as she stood up and walked off to the toilet. I followed her, mad that Katy could have been so insensitive. As usual Katy had overstepped the mark and a fun conversation had ended up in someone getting hurt.

"Are you ok?" I asked Jenny.

"She had no right to say that."

"No, she didn't."

"Who does she think she is?"

By the time we got back to the table everyone was getting up to dance – apart from Katy. I caught her eye and shook my head slowly letting her know exactly what I thought. To Jenny's credit she sat back down, and Katy immediately tried to apologize.

"I'm really sorry, Jenny. I didn't think about what I was saying. I'm really sorry. It's a problem I have sometimes in that I just don't think."

I was surprised that Katy wasn't trying to justify what she had said and hoped Jenny would accept her apology and allow the night to move on. Jenny clearly wasn't feeling forgiving and said it was ok, but made her excuses and left.

"Why did you have to say that?" I asked Katy when Jenny had gone.

"I don't know, it was just what I was thinking. I know I shouldn't have but I didn't expect her to react like that. Maybe I hit a nerve?"

"Maybe you did, but I wish you'd kept your bloody mouth shut."

"You never know, I might have made her think about her relationship and now they might make more of an effort. Perhaps good will come out of it?"

"I think the most that will come out of it is that she'll never want to see you again and that she's lying awake thinking about the possibility of Simon having an affair. Well, it's the first time I've seen you care that you might have hurt someone so I guess that's a good thing."

"Oh come on, Alice, don't be like that."

I didn't need to say anymore. I knew she hadn't thought. That was Katy. She just came right out with whatever she was thinking. In one way you always knew where you stood and she was transparent, but in another she could cut to the very heart of you.

# CHAPTER TWENTY-ONE

Over the following weeks I thought a lot about our drunken conversation that had ended with Jenny leaving early. From the start I had wanted to include sex and relationship problems in my column and now my urge was even stronger. I wasn't sure how to approach it with the editor, knowing that she wasn't really keen on the idea. Even though she wanted us to get closer to our readers I knew she hadn't envisaged getting quite so intimate, and was happy with the way the advice pages were running. But we needed to reflect more of the issues that were really affecting people and it was an area I felt we needed to tread.

I spent my spare time doing some research so that I could approach her from a position of strength, to sound like I knew what I was talking about. I scanned through lots of women's magazines to find out what the current trends were regarding one of the most taboo subjects in the world. Flicking through most of the glossies made me feel like I was stuck in a time warp. Was having a great multiple orgasm really at the top of most women's wants when it came to sex? Was that all we really cared about?

I wondered if it was just my group of friends who weren't having sex anymore, but guessed we were just a small percentage of a much larger statistic. More women than ever before were trying to juggle a career and cope with the family, and men were suffering more emotionally as the pressure to keep their jobs rose. It was obvious that stress affected the intimacy of a relationship and I wondered how many couples were avoiding the one thing that could bring them closer together.

The more I read the more I realized how superficially the subject was being dealt with. I spent night after night wading through the internet to try and find what I was looking for. I kept thinking about the issue of intimacy. It was as if it was being ignored, but wasn't there a huge amount of women who craved intimacy above all else? Weren't we wired differently, and didn't we need to feel loved before we really enjoyed having sex?

After trailing through magazine and newspaper articles, trend dossiers and statistical data I came to the conclusion that thirty-plus women weren't being catered for. There were so many issues affecting mums, yet they weren't being discussed in a way that could help to alleviate some of the problems. How did they bring intimacy back into a marriage that was embedded with stressful situations and rekindle the fire that once ignited them? How could they bring more balance into their lives so that they did have time for pleasurable things? I also wondered if I was one of the minorities who actually feared sex altogether, viewing it as anything but pleasurable.

I compiled a proposal for my editor, in an attempt to delve a bit deeper into some of the real issues affecting people. I left the proposal with her and waited for her response.

It was over two weeks before I got an answer, and I feared I'd pushed my luck with the suggestions that I'd made. We had a formal meeting and she made it clear that she wanted anything but sex advice in my column. I felt myself go red, as if I had suggested the worst possible idea, but with all the effort I had put in I didn't want to give up easily.

"I would be happy to just focus on issues relating to intimacy if that sits better with you?" I suggested, in the hope of salvaging at least part of my idea.

"But won't that just lead to sex advice anyway?"

"No. There can be way more to it than just sex. I'd like to focus on things like getting back to being honest with each other as a starting point to bringing back real intimacy into a relationship."

"Why do I get the feeling your time is up on this paper?" she suddenly said.

"What do you mean?" I said, frightened that I had gone too far, and was about to face redundancy – a fear that loomed without pushing ideas that weren't welcomed.

"I think you should be working for a magazine – not a local paper. I just can't offer you the scope of what you really want to do."

"But I love my job, I understand if my proposal isn't in line with your editorial stance. It was only a suggestion. I'm happy for it not to be incorporated." I suddenly felt like I was fighting for my job.

"Don't look so worried, Alice, I know you love your job, but you've been more passionate about this proposal than anything you've ever written about since you started here. I really don't want to lose you, but I think you're going to naturally drift away. I can't offer you what you really want to write about and think you could fly somewhere else."

I was taken aback by what she had said and tried as hard as I could to convince her of how happy I was, but I got the feeling she was already planning who could take over from me.

The next week was torture – coming into the office everyday not knowing if it would be my last. I found myself working harder than ever in the hope of overturning the decision I felt she had already made.

It was three weeks to the day of our dreaded conversation when she popped her head around the door of my office and asked if I had five minutes. I feared what I was about to hear and assumed the worst. I had hoped that it wouldn't happen – putting my head in the sand and hoping for the best. I knocked on her door and waited. I kept my eyes to the floor to avoid having to engage with anyone that might walk past. Paranoia set in as I realized how naive I had been.

"Come in," she said after a few minutes. As I opened the door I took a deep breath in preparation for the blow that was about to be dealt to me. I sat down opposite her.

"I've been thinking. I've got a good friend who's just been promoted to Deputy Editor of Isis magazine. I think it's the perfect platform for you. If it's something that appeals to you I could arrange for you to meet her?"

I couldn't believe what I was hearing. I had assumed the complete opposite and my reaction mimicked my surprise. I looked at her without saying anything – part of me thought I'd misheard what she had said and I felt self-conscious not really knowing how to respond. A few seconds later, after internally relaying what I had heard, I suddenly felt relief. I wasn't being made redundant. It took a few minutes more for what she was saying to sink in. I wasn't sure how to react to her offer, wondering if she was testing my loyalty to the paper.

"It dawned on me last night that where she wants to take the magazine and what you have proposed to me have a lot of synergy."

"If you think she'd be happy to talk to me, I'd love to. It just feels uncomfortable agreeing to it when I'm really happy here."

"I just think it could be a really great opportunity for you. I'll call her tonight, and then you can take it from there."

As I walked back to my desk, pangs of insecurity plagued me. The fear that I was being set up was hard to ignore and I tried to fight the feelings that she was just trying to get rid of me. For the rest of the afternoon I swung between believing she was genuinely trying to help me, to feeling stupid for even thinking that she would put me before the paper. I couldn't fathom why she would offer me a potential lead to another job if she really wanted me to stay working for her. Something definitely wasn't right and I found it impossible to concentrate as I tried to figure out what was going on.

The following three days were consumed by what felt like an extended anxiety attack. Normally when I got home from work I couldn't wait to see the kids and spend time with them, but something had changed in me and as I tried to listen to them talking about their day all I could think about was my job. I couldn't focus on anything they were saying. Paranoia had set in and I started to believe that the supposed offer of another potential job was a ruse to make me redundant from my current one.

I was slightly lifted when an actual meeting was scheduled for me to meet the Deputy Editor of Isis, but felt sunken soon after feeling sure it was a ploy to lessen the blow of me being made redundant. I convinced myself that it was a way of giving me hope and an opportunity to be offered some advice about finding another job.

The next shock came a day later in a letter from Sam's solicitor. He had declared bankruptcy, claiming that any assets we had collectively owned were now out of his control. He agreed to pay minimal child maintenance but expressed regret that that was all he could offer. Deep down I had known he would do all he could to ensure that he siphoned every penny that could possibly be rewarded to myself and the children. It was a price I had been willing to pay and now I knew that I had to say goodbye to all the financial investment I had put into our relationship. Despite the financial insecurity that loomed over me, I was now in control of my life and leaving Sam meant more than anything else. Despite my impending redundancy I felt sure I would find another job to support us.

The day before my meeting at Isis I decided to think positively and focus on selling myself, in the hope that I might be offered some freelance work. Once the children were tucked up in bed, I took some time out to read through a copy of Isis. It was a glossy, stylish magazine with an editorial policy that didn't believe in puff pieces – its ethos was to get to the heart of women's issues – in the most elegant way. It was catering for a female readership who loved looking stylish but also wanted more. As I flicked through the pages it was obvious what a brilliant balance they'd reached between interesting lifestyle advice, to in-depth articles that were genuinely trying to make a difference to people's lives. They had won so many awards for their research and campaigns – often focusing on subjects that other magazines had never dared to go near. I was excited about meeting Lara and felt the pressure of what to wear. I knew the snobbery that went with working for a national magazine and was determined to look the part.

# CHAPTER TWENTY-TWO

I felt daunted as I stared up at the building that towered above me. Isis was part of a huge publishing empire and I headed for the twenty-first floor. The views were amazing as the glass lift climbed upwards, allowing me to look down on the breathtaking sites of London. Part of me loved living in the countryside, but London offered so much more.

Clutching a folder full of press clippings, I sat in the reception and waited for Lara to greet me. I peered through the translucent wall and watched everyone working in the open-plan office. It seemed like a more relaxed atmosphere than my office and everyone was dressed so much more casually than I had expected.

As Lara appeared I was surprised by her appearance. I imagined her to be tall, very smartly dressed with dark hair. Instead she was small, wearing jeans with beautiful auburn hair that was tossed into a half-hearted ponytail that looked like it would fall out at any minute. She wasn't wearing any shoes.

"Hi, you must be Alice," she said with a big smile. "I'm Lara, it's good to meet you. I'm having my monthly purge so you'll have to excuse the mess when we get inside my office. There's paper everywhere I'm afraid."

I followed her across the large open office as we headed for a door that was covered in photos. She could see my surprise.

"I couldn't stand the color of the door, so instead of painting it I decided to stick photos of everyone who works here. It's gonna end up looking like the wall of shame."

As I scanned the pictures I realized what she meant. There had obviously been some wild nights out and some heavy drinking sessions in the office that whilst initially private were now on view to everyone.

"Come in and have a seat. Tanya's told me a bit about you, she seems really impressed by everything you've done at the paper. I'm not sure if she made it clear why I wanted to meet you?"

I didn't want to undersell myself in being honest about why I thought I was there so I tried to cautiously answer her.

"Tanya mentioned there was some synergy between some of the ideas I had put forward to her and where you're planning to take Isis."

"Yes, it seems like it. I was running some ideas past her as I always do, and suddenly she stopped me and said you had proposed some ideas to her that were exactly along the lines of what I wanted to do."

Suddenly I felt comfortable, realizing that just perhaps Tanya had been genuine all along in actually wanting to help me.

"I want to go more in-depth with the way we cover sex in the magazine. We've got to give our readers more than the best positions to spice up their love life. The last article we ran about getting more in touch with our femininity got such great feedback that I know there's so much more we need to cover. We want to be able to relate more to women's emotions and what's really going on behind closed doors. As a genre we seem to be fixated on which are the right buttons to encourage men to press but if the environment isn't conducive they're never really going to be triggered properly. I want to focus more on what intimacy really means and how we can help people rekindle the love that they felt when they first fell in love."

I could feel myself glowing as I listened to what she was saying. It was too good to be true that my proposal to Tanya covered the same things as what she wanted to do.

"I think you'll appreciate how busy I am, so I don't think you'll be surprised to know that I asked Tanya for your proposal so that I could read it myself before asking you to come and see me. It would have been a waste of both our time if your style and vision wasn't in-line with where the magazine is heading."

Suddenly I felt like I was in a job interview. It was the last thing I had thought about in coming to see her but it felt fantastic. The best I had hoped for was some possible freelance work, but the more she spoke the more it felt like she was actually considering me for a full-time position.

"What I'm looking for is to go beyond just talking about sex and broaden the subject to cover all the real issues surrounding it. Getting to the heart of the matter is what we're all about and it's time we went more in-depth. To do it justice I need to take on a full-time features writer to focus on the subject. I've always believed the best writing comes from journalists being fully imbedded in the culture of the magazine – living and breathing it every day and being part of the team."

"What an amazing opportunity," I said, still unsure if I was being considered for the position or had misread the signs completely. "It sounds like my perfect job. God, I feel guilty saying that."

"Tanya set this meeting up didn't she? You know how incestuous this industry is. I honestly can't remember the last time I didn't recruit through someone I know."

"I don't want to sound presumptuous but I had no idea there was a job opening on Isis that you might be considering me for?" I cringed after I'd said it, but I needed to be clear about what was going on.

"I like you, I like the work I've seen and there's no question that you and your writing style would fit in perfectly here. Perhaps the next step is for me to fill you in on a bit about the magazine, let you meet the team and see how it feels for you. Then I'd like to give you a project to complete before we take anything further."

We spent over two hours together, with her doing most of the talking, and me listening trying to take everything in. I was introduced to the staff, and just before I left she set me an assignment that she wanted me to submit by the end of the week. I agreed that I'd write a 2000-word feature on a specific topic that she would email me the following day.

I was buzzing with excitement as I left the office. As I stared out of the lift the view looked amazing. It was a bright, cold day and I caught a glimpse of two of the bridges that crossed the River Thames. How stunning London looked on a clear day. The thought of working in the city felt so exciting and although it would mean a lot of juggling where the children were concerned, I knew I could make it work. It had been a long time since something had felt too good to be true, but the potential opportunity to work at Isis felt like that.

I found a cafe that looked really inviting. The atmosphere was amazing, as the sounds of loud chatter echoed throughout its high ceilings. I sat myself down on a comfy sofa and read through some of the back issues of Isis. The magazine really was the epitome of cool, yet it had a heart and was genuinely interested in trying to make a difference to the lives of its readers, rather than just trying to sell things to them. I hated the magazines that had sold out to their advertisers. Obviously advertisers were key to their survival but the balance had long disappeared between the editorial they offered and what they were trying to sell. I felt so excited but was also waiting for the fall and expected it to come once I had submitted my article. It was hard to think that less than a year before I had almost given up on life – the contrast of what possibly lay ahead of me just seemed too surreal to comprehend. I would be writing about a subject that I was passionate about – mainly because I was so desperate to find it in my own life. I had experienced the extreme of a relationship that lacked emotional intimacy, where violence had taken the place of any form of physical affection, and deep down wanted to experience a relationship that was based on love, of wanting the best for one another rather than encouraging the worst.

People were right when they said my experience with Sam would make me stronger. At the time I thought it was the most insensitive thing anyone could have said to me. If strength really came from such a shit deal then I would rather have swapped it for being weak. But there was no denying that the whole experience had forced me to think about what really mattered to me, and standing up for myself had without doubt unleashed a side of me that would have stayed buried if it wasn't for all that I had gone through.

I left the café and walked passed a clinic that was offering acupuncture and hypnotherapy and thought that it was perhaps time to deal with what I hoped was one of the last of my demons. I still feared the thought of having sex, and it was one of the reasons that I had kept a distance from any opportunity to have a relationship again. With the prospect of a potential new job I had to get over the one thing that was stopping me from finding love in my life. I knew I couldn't do it by myself – I could write about it and have banter with my friends but I was inwardly terrified of letting anyone get close to me – let alone getting intimate. Friends and family had tried to set me up – there had been a few dates but I couldn't let anyone hurt me again. My barriers were up and I couldn't work out how to get them down again.

I felt like having fun that evening, as I walked through the door and realized the boys were already in bed. Perhaps it was wrong to admit that it was a relief that I didn't have to be mum and they had been taken care of. I kissed my mum goodbye and gave her a hug that would be hard for her to understand. It was full of emotion that words couldn't convey. I felt cared for in a way that I couldn't express as I wiped back tears trying not to let her see. Life felt great again. I called Katy hoping she could come over.

"Do you fancy coming to mine tonight? Let's get a takeaway and wine and have a catch up."

"Sounds good to me, what time shall I come over?"

"Whenever you like, the kids are already asleep."

"Brill, I'll be over in half an hour, with a takeaway. Our usual I take it?"

"Oh yes. For God's sake don't forget the mango chutney."

"I did it once and now you bloody remind me every time."

"Sorry it's just not the same without it."

"I know, I know. I'll make sure it's there, Alice. See you later."

Katy's timing was perfect. The boys were fast asleep and I'd even had time to have a bath. I was ready for a girls' night in and poured two glasses of wine in anticipation of Katy's arrival.

Our conversations always covered so many things but we spent most of the night talking about my potential new job and how much Katy wanted to get out of hers. She had worked in PR for fifteen years, and was secretly hoping to be made redundant. She was confident she could get another job using her skills in a different field, and was just waiting to be told they would have to let her go.

Then we got onto the subject that always caused her to get cross with me. Whenever we talked about relationships Katy always closed off. She loved being single and wanted it to stay that way.

"Honestly, have you ever really, really loved someone?" I asked her as we neared the end of our second bottle of wine.

"Oh God, Alice, I hate it when you ask me these sorts of questions. What the hell do you mean?"

"Oh come on. You know what I mean. Have you ever felt for someone so much love that you'd do anything for them?"

"What? You're trying to use me as some bloody case study for a future article aren't you?"

"No, I'm genuinely interested. It's only a question you don't need to get so defensive."

"Of course I have. I really, really love Jane. I'd do anything for her, you know I would."

"I know that. I meant a man. Have you ever been properly in love? Were you ever completely in love with Steve?"

"Course I was or I wouldn't have married him. I loved him for over ten years before I realized we had nothing in common and I was more like his mother than a wife."

She went to the toilet, came back into the living room and threw a cushion at me from the sofa.

"Oh my God, I can't believe you're now getting me to question if I ever actually loved Steve. Do you know what, if I'm being really honest I thought I really loved him at first, but then the relationship probably became more convenient than anything else and he annoyed me more than I felt love for him."

"I know I never really loved Sam, and I bloody married him. I spent more time hating him than anything else. At the beginning I was totally taken in by him, but I wasn't actually in love with him. There was too much about him that I didn't like, but I just tried to ignore it and then, well it just all got out of control."

"Blimey, doesn't it feel like such a long time ago that you were with him? Thank God you got away from him. I hate that bastard, if I ever saw him again I'd tell him exactly what I thought."

"I don't want to think about him anymore. Hopefully he's out of our lives forever now. It still affects me sometimes you know, and I'm never sure what to say to the boys. I still get anxiety attacks every time I think about him seeking his revenge on me. It feels so uncomfortable that he's just disappeared – I just know he's up to something."

"I don't think you should worry anymore. Surely if he was going to try something he would have done it by now?"

"You don't know Sam. He never left anything unfinished with anyone he believed had betrayed him. It sounds sick but he would plan how to get back at them and I still live in fear of what he might try and do to me or the kids."

"You've got to try and forget about him, Alice. Maybe he's with someone else now and wants to forget about you and the kids. That would be the best situation wouldn't it?"

"It would be for me, but I worry about them growing up not knowing their dad."

"In the long run it will be so much better for them that they don't have him in their lives, and you never know, you might meet someone soon?"

"I so want to experience what it would be like to be completely and utterly in love with someone. To love everything about them, and feel it back from them too."

"Sometimes I think you're twelve," Katy snapped at me. "You remind me of a little girl dreaming about finding her prince charming. What part of life did you miss out on that showed you that fairytales aren't real? You of all people should realize that."

"Perhaps it's because I've experienced everything that love wasn't that I now want to know what it could be like. Look, I've known the depths of hate; you can't knock me for wanting to feel the heights of love. It's written about in every love song – I'm not the only one searching you know."

# CHAPTER TWENTY-THREE

I woke up with an awful hangover, but still managed to laugh about the heated conversation Katy and I had had the previous evening. We were such opposites but that's what made it such fun being together. I got the kids to school on time and went into work with a completely new perspective, being so grateful to Tanya for the introduction to Isis. She had heard my meeting with Lara was a success, and said matter-of-factly that if I was formally offered a job, Lara had agreed to a six-week handover, giving me time to train up the deputy features editor before I left. It seemed so mature the way my current boss was talking to me about my prospective new job, and I still couldn't properly digest the opportunity that had appeared in front of me. Yes, it was happening to me, but I felt I was outside of the experience watching it occur.

As promised, there was an email waiting for me from Lara as I opened my inbox. It was a warm email saying it was good to meet me and that she had had time to think about a header for the feature she would like me to write. I scanned down to see what she had come up with: 'Why the object of our desire isn't each other anymore.' I sat and thought about what the title actually meant and how I could approach it.

At the first opportunity, once the kids were in bed, I sat down to start the article. My first stop was to find statistics to support what I was going to write. I laughed at myself as I tried to find data to back up my argument – what was it about journalists and their love of statistics? Why were statistics so important when most were the result of very costly PR campaigns? Of course, you could find legitimate stats that hadn't been created with a company's product in mind, but you needed to know your source, and not get drawn into those that were notorious for their spin. I searched until I finally found a source to help give my feature the foundation I wanted.

After a few nights sat at the computer I was finally happy with what I had written. I was ready to email the article to Lara. I felt self-conscious about sending it, worried that I may not meet the standard she was expecting. That was the problem with writing for a new audience – I'd become so comfortable on the newspaper, but this was a different challenge altogether. I hoped I'd hit the mark and knew it was riding on me being offered the job. I pressed send and tried not to think about the possible rejection that could come with what I had written.

When I walked into the newspaper a few days later, Tanya came straight into my office as if she had been waiting for me.

"I hear Lara was impressed with your article."

"Was she?" I answered, surprised that I hadn't heard from her myself.

"She asked for your home number last night, I thought she would have called you?"

"No, she didn't."

"Why don't you call her? Come back to me after you've spoken to her."

I couldn't wait to call her. It was one thing hearing from Tanya that she liked what I'd written but another from Lara herself.

"Hi, Lara, it's Alice. Hope you don't mind me calling you but I understand you spoke to Tanya about the article I wrote."

"Hi, good to hear from you. Listen, I loved it and want to run with it in the magazine. I think I told you we work three months ahead of ourselves so we go to print next week with the magazine that your article will appear in. We've made a few tweaks that will be emailed over to you. Can you put together some short bullet points to add to the feature that offer a summary of the main suggestions in the article?"

"Yes, of course. I'll get them over to you by end of play

tomorrow, if that's ok?"

"Great. Let me get this magazine to bed and then come in so that we can dot the i's and cross the t's. I'd like to offer you the job, have you decided if it's what you want to do?"

"Yes," I said without any hesitation. "I can't wait. Thank you so much for this opportunity."

"Ok, I'll get a contract drawn up. We haven't spoken about salary yet. I'm not sure what you take home at the moment but what we offer is pretty standard, but it might be slightly less than you're used to. I'll find out what the salary is and get back to you."

I had already decided it didn't matter what salary they offered me. The job was too good an opportunity to turn down because of the money. I knew I could get by and if it meant cutting back then that's what I'd have to do.

The next few days felt like the start of a new chapter in my life. I had more energy, more enthusiasm and I couldn't wait to start at Isis. I looked around the house and realized how much clutter I had accumulated over the past few years. It felt like the right time to get rid of anything that we didn't need or hadn't used in a while.

There were lots of surprises in store that evening as I rummaged through boxes that I had kept at my parents' house for years. Finding things I didn't know I owned was fun for the first hour – until I realized how much rubbish I had actually hoarded. The best part was getting sidetracked by old photos. As I flicked through photo albums that were so old they were literally falling apart, I felt like I was being transported back to the scene of every picture that I looked at. As I worked my way through an album dedicated to my first love, Mark, the memories came flooding back of the happy times we had spent together. There was such an innocence about the way we loved one another. It was a very special time for me and one that I had never forgotten about. I used to reminisce all the time about him and all the fun we had shared together, but while I was with Sam it became too difficult to think about Mark, wondering how life could have been if we had stayed together. I had often thought that perhaps it was just down to how young we were – that we were naive and hadn't yet been tainted by the world – but I knew in my heart I had never felt the same love for anyone else. Our relationship had been magical and so uncomplicated. It was if for the four years we were together we were engulfed in a bubble of love, that couldn't be penetrated or popped by anything or anyone.

Tucked in the back of a photo album were love letters Mark had written to me. He had been at boarding school for a year whilst we were together, and from what I gathered we must have written to each other virtually every day whilst he was there. I had kept at least sixty of the letters and sat and read each one. I was tearful as I read the beautiful words that he had written to me, and guessed I must have matched his passion in the ones I wrote back to him. We were so open about how we felt for one another and I wondered if I could ever really be that way with anyone else again. There was no fear of being hurt, and we didn't judge one another. The more I read, the more I realized how well suited we were. I felt like I was acknowledging for the first time in my life the void that had been left when Mark and I had split up. It had hurt so much but at the time it seemed like there was no other solution. I was going off to university at the other end of the country and he had been offered a job where he had to work at weekends. It seemed impossible for us to see each other, and so, reluctantly he had ended our relationship, saying it couldn't work anymore. I was devastated, but the excitement of going off to university carried me through the initial painful stages of us splitting up.

Over time I had blocked out of my consciousness the amazing bond and love that we had shared together and went on my way to try and recreate the experience with someone else. As I closed the album, I sat and cried. There was a yearning to know how he was and what he was doing. He suddenly felt like the best friend I had lost and wanted to find again.

# CHAPTER TWENTY-FOUR

Over the next few days I couldn't stop thinking about Mark and the intimacy we had enjoyed together. The more I thought about that time in my life the more I realized how much I had changed after I met Sam. At the beginning, when he had made me feel loved, there had never been a problem between us. But as his love turned into the need to control me, everything started to change. The signs were there, staring me in the face, but I ignored them, hankering after a lifestyle that I believed would replace my need for intimacy. To all the outsiders his abuse towards me was obvious very early on in our relationship, but I took his assaults personally and started to believe the awful things he said about me. The biggest cracks started to appear when I felt like he was using me for a quick fix – I needed more when we were in bed together, and he couldn't give it to me. It was as if without feeling loved I couldn't perform – literally. I didn't see it that way at the time and believed I had a serious problem. Whenever we tried to have sex it became impossible, and as the pain of trying got worse – so did our relationship. It got so bad, that despite my embarrassment I went to see a doctor, but regretted ever doing so as he didn't know how to deal with me. He made me feel even worse, like I was suffering from a frigid disease. Try a vibrator, he suggested. I walked out shameful wishing I had never gone to see him.

That's when I spiraled into depression. I was dead inside and didn't know how to ignite myself. Then the vicious circle started where Sam felt like I was rejecting him. Instead of trying to be understanding, realizing I had a problem, he started on the road of trying to physically force me to have sex with him. The pain was indescribable and I started to hate my body for getting me into the terrible situations I suddenly found myself in. The more forceful Sam became the more out of control I started to feel, and the more fearful I became about having sex. I began to feel worthless and as a consequence instead of standing up for myself, submitted more to him, suffering silently biting my lips through the horrendous ordeal. Never had I imagined it would get to the point where it was no longer about trying to have sex with me but wanting to physically punish me instead.

The fear from that part of my life was definitely the main reason why I was frightened of entering into another relationship – yet I knew more than anything that I wanted to find real love again. Remembering the amazing connection that Mark and I enjoyed together gave me hope that when I met the right person I would overcome my fear, but I couldn't help wishing it was him I would reunite with.

Mark and I were the first for each other when it came to losing our virginity. I had been brainwashed as a child by my Catholic upbringing and had no intention of finding out about the supposed joys of sex until I was married. He had respected and tolerated my outdated beliefs until a night when we had both had too much to drink. The intensity between us was too great for me to hold back, and as we both ventured into pastures new I couldn't end the passion that fuelled us to carry on. Afterwards I was plagued by guilt for what I had done and wasn't sure I could bring myself to do it again. I felt I had cursed myself and would be damned for what I had allowed to happen. Mark found it hard to understand why I felt so awful about what we had done, and I tried to explain to him about my Sunday school education. I remember him sitting in disbelief as I told him about a friend who had stood up and asked how babies were made. It happened when I was about nine and she asked the priest how her mum and dad had made her baby brother. We all giggled but the priest launched into a monologue about the sinful side of sex, telling us how one used it to produce children but for anything else they would be going against God's will and for that they would be punished. He even went as far as to warn us about the urges we would get as we grew up.

"Your body will try and lure you away from being pure for God," I remembered him saying. Over time he had bashed away at our subconscious, and the result – sex was bad. God punished those who used it for means other than to produce children.

Mark had shocked me about his views towards sex – it was as if our opinions were the extremes of one and other, and as a result he would always provoke me. He once challenged me saying that if God didn't want us to enjoy sex then why did orgasms feel so good. I couldn't answer him. He believed God loved everyone and didn't judge and was the first person to introduce me to the idea that sex was a spiritual practice in the East. He was much more open minded than your average eighteen-year-old due to the time he had spent in India, staying with his way-out auntie who had married a yogi and moved to the base of the Himalayas. He loved his trips there and always returned a more mature version of the boy who had left a month before. He always stimulated my mind, especially after he had been in India. There was something calming about the confidence is his beliefs, and after a while I started to realize how dogmatic my religion had become. Yes, we were offered hope, but only if we followed the rule. It was as if we were encouraged to idealize the very people that made us feel bad about ourselves, and that in itself no longer sat comfortably with me.

Thinking about Mark and the conversations we used to have gave me an idea for a possible feature for Isis. Sex and religion was something I felt we needed to cover and I wanted to interview heads of various faiths to find out their differences of opinions, as well as what they agreed on when it came to God's rule about sex.

I emailed my idea to Lara the following evening and wondered how she would react to it. A few days later she called, enthusiastic about my suggestion.

"I love it, but need you to expand what you're planning. I

want you to cover different countries' cultural views too. Then I want us to do a poll out on the streets. I want a survey of a thousand women. I want to know their views. I want an interview with a representative from every religion you can think of. Don't stop at the obvious ones, include everyone. It's about time we covered this sort of stuff."

I liked her idea about going out on the street and wondered how many outdated beliefs were still stuck in the consciousness of the country. The religious hold was definitely starting to lift, but were we still being brainwashed to feel bad about ourselves? No one could deny that as a culture our obsession with sex was at an all-time high, but was it due to how much we had been repressed? Wasn't it natural that when you were told something was bad it made it all the more alluring? Perhaps my obsession to write about sex came from my own denial when I was younger, but I knew there were thousands like me, potentially millions who as a child had been influenced so much that they were still carrying guilt.

We agreed that I would start to work on the feature the day I joined the magazine. I thought about all the religions I could approach, and wondered how similar or different they would be in their attitudes towards sex. Would they even talk to me, I wondered? But I gathered they would, based on the fact that most of them had their own PR people, trained for the sole purpose of coming across well in the media.

As I started to think about the immense wealth behind some of the world's most prominent religions I wondered what they were doing to help their people at a time when job loss was so high, rather than just preaching to them. A cynic on the radio a few days before had referred to religion as the best recession-proof business in the world, and although it was a harsh attack on something that offered hope to so many, you couldn't help thinking about how bureaucratic and corrupt so many religions had become.

# CHAPTER TWENTY-FIVE

It was great to start at Isis. My desk was the last of a row of five people, and they all seemed friendly trying to make me feel comfortable on my first day. The atmosphere was so relaxed, and I found it hard to get used to people shouting across the office. At my previous job it went against office etiquette to even talk to the person sitting next to you, let alone shout to someone instead of using the internal phone system. At Isis everyone seemed oblivious to the phone or walking over to someone to ask them a question, and no one seemed to care if you needed to concentrate. After a few days I realized that the noise went in waves. The mornings seemed to be the worst times, with a lull during the main part of the day when everyone seemed to be silent, and then in the late afternoon the atmosphere relaxed again.

The research that went with my first feature kept me really busy, and my findings started to point towards religion's negative attitude towards sex. If it wasn't bad enough that Catholicism made you wait until you were married, it did its damnedest to ensure you didn't enjoy it when you were finally granted bail. It wasn't until the mid-1960s that America had legalized birth control – heavy lobbying from the Catholic Church was the main reason why it had stayed illegal for so long. Whilst the UK offered contraception to women who were married in the early 1960s, it wasn't until the 1970s that you could legally obtain birth control if you weren't married. Didn't that go a long way to ensure people were terrified of sex? Imagine feeling like you couldn't protect yourself? You'd hardly enjoy the act when an unwanted child could be the consequence. Wasn't the idea of contraception to allow women to enjoy themselves without the pressure of pregnancy?

I suggested to Lara that we included an Indian tantra master to run alongside the rest of the interviews. Technically it was more a philosophy and spiritual practice but it seemed to have a natural place as an opposed opinion to the general consensus.

"It's not really mainstream, Alice? I think it might do more harm than good if we include it alongside other religious and cultural beliefs."

"Maybe it could be a separate interview for an article at a later date?"

"Actually, we could run with a feature on tantra for the February edition – start thinking about some of the celebrities who swear by it."

I learned very quickly that Lara was always five steps ahead of the rest of us and very direct with her instructions. It made my job easy in that I never had to second guess what she expected, but meant I was always thinking about a million things at once.

In an editorial meeting it was decided that we would invite readers to write in off the back of the feature to get an idea of the differing viewpoints we were catering for. The best letter would be published and the winner would receive £500 worth of clothes and beauty vouchers. You were always guaranteed good feedback when you offered something in return for a letter, and our advertisers clamored at the opportunity of additional coverage.

Perhaps it was the £500 reward – but we received more letters in response to that article than any other piece Isis had ever run. The subject was a hot potato and we had only stumbled on the tip of it. There were some angry responses claiming never to buy the magazine again, saying how ashamed they were that we had taken such a high-street approach to people that were so spiritual in nature. Their anger seemed to arise from the slant that we had taken. We were inferring that religion as a whole had made us feel bad about our bodies and a natural fun act had been turned into one of the most sinful things anyone could do. Perhaps it wasn't that extreme anymore, but we insinuated that the damage had been done and we were now stumbling in the dark as a culture not really sure of what we should and shouldn't be enjoying.

We put the angry letters in the 'Sex As Sin' box. Harsh perhaps, but we could see the conditioning these people were under just from what they had written – so-called religious people who were so judgmental of everyone else it was actually quite scary to read their letters. Then there were the 'I hate what religion is doing to this world' responses. They were passionate and thoughtful and cared deeply about where the world was headed. Then, to our surprise, the vast majority of letters were stories of women's own personal experiences.

We were stunned by their honesty and obvious confusion over a subject that got more media coverage, alongside violence, than anything else. There was an obvious trend and it was startling. Woman felt like objects and misunderstood their sexuality and how they could actually feel happy about it. The winner stood out by a long shot. She was a professional sex therapist and she told the story of how she had ended up in such a role. We turned her letter into a profile, including her picture and contact information at the end.

Four weeks later she told us she was amazed by the surge of new clients that had called her after reading her feature in the magazine. It was obvious we would benefit from her input. At an editorial meeting we talked about her writing ad hoc articles. I called her and suggested an informal tie-up. She jumped at the chance and offered us more than we expected.

"There's a subject you have to cover," she said. "One in five of my female clients have some form of sexual dysfunction and they can't get the help to solve the problem. They come to me as a last resort."

"This is closer to home than you could ever imagine," I said, wanting to be honest with her. "It's something I've been through myself. I know exactly what you're talking about."

"Then cover it in the magazine. It's a real issue that isn't being talked about. Get it out in the open, help people not to feel so ostracized."

Lara was sold on the idea and I started looking for statistics to back up what we would write about. It didn't take long to find the facts. Whilst there was no British statistical data, America offered some interesting information. According to the American Medical Journal, 43% of women suffered from some form of sexual dysfunction. Viagra had given voice to the male trend but the statistics were higher for women and no one was talking about the problem. The cynical side of me believed it was because a female equivalent to Viagra hadn't yet been launched. I had no doubt that as and when it was ready the same coverage would be granted to female issues, like it had been for men.

Our judgment was right to run the feature and the result was thousands of heartfelt letters. The magazine had a policy to reply to every letter we received but the amount that flooded in made it impossible to respond to every single one. We were amazed at how many people were suffering in silence, not knowing where to turn to without the worry of being ridiculed. We decided to set up a panel of experts that could answer all of the queries that people had written to us about and ran a six-page feature dealing with all the issues that had been raised. We had a sex therapist, doctor, psychologist, hypnotherapist, marital counsellor and gynecologist, all offering their expertise and advice.

Off the back of that article I received a confidential letter from a celebrity who felt very strongly about the subject and offered to speak out about her personal experience. Lara asked me to make contact with her and arrange an interview to run in a future edition.

The interview was more eye opening than I had expected, and by the end of our conversation she had referred me to her friend who had also suffered. This friend was a famous singer in her own right and I was surprised when she mentioned her name.

"I'm stunned that she's had problems," I said.

"Why?" said my interviewee.

"Because she oozes sexuality."

"On the outside maybe, but that's just an image that's been created for her. It wasn't the truth for a long time, but she's over it now. She doesn't care what people think and would be happy to talk to you."

I thanked her for the interview and her honesty and then went and told Lara about our potential additional interviewee. She wanted her to be included and, as I suspected, asked me to set up the interview as soon as possible.

"I want women to know that even celebrities who supposedly have everything, have deep emotional issues too," she said.

"Ok, I'll contact her tomorrow and get the interview tied up."

On my way to the station that evening I saw a flyer in the window of the yoga studio opposite our office. It was brightly colored and the title caught my eye: 'Love Like You've Never Been Hurt', a lecture and workshop by Tibetan Lama, Osi Kusum Yoka. I went closer to read the small print. 'This is the first and only time His Holiness Osi Kusum Yoka will address a UK audience. Offering ancient wisdom to help heal your past, you will be taken on a journey inwards that will change your life forever.' Bold words I thought for a two-hour lecture, but I was intrigued. I initially justified my fascination by thinking it would be good fodder for a future article – but deep down I knew it was for me.

I booked my ticket the following day and told Lara I was going.

"I'm not sure about that kind of philosophy," she said when I told her what it was about. "I don't want to run an article on him, but let me know if anything interesting comes out of it that we could include."

As I arrived at the auditorium I was surprised by how many people were there. It was a huge theatre and virtually every seat was taken. Just after I sat down, our speaker appeared on the stage. He was a small man, and I was amazed at how quiet the audience became as he stood in front of them. His voice was much bigger than his physical presence and although quite soft in its tone sounded very authoritative as he spoke into the microphone. He introduced himself and then without literally wasting a second launched into a monologue that lasted about fifteen minutes. Having forgotten my Dictaphone, I tried to write down everything that he was saying but it was hard to keep up using the shorthand that often failed me.

"Love is not handed on a plate," he said with a strong Asian accent that echoed throughout the huge auditorium. "It is something you have to work at, want to strive to achieve. For all of you who have made it to the boardroom – you have had to work hard and ensure your voice is heard. For those of you who have the demanding job of looking after your children, you have had to find your boundaries, work at sticking to them, and learn on the job what it means to responsibly bring up children. Please imagine love to be the same thing. It doesn't just happen. Mr. Right might well come along but how long will you think of him as your prince charming? And what is actually right for you, if you haven't focused on yourself and got rid of the parts that weren't even you in the first place."

He could tell that most of the audience was confused by what he said and tried to explain himself more clearly.

"I am not talking about body parts. What I talk about are the parts of your personality that have developed out of being hurt, that you can get rid of. How many people want to change something about themselves?"

Everyone put up their hands and he carried on talking.

"We've all been hurt. Some more than others but a natural defense is to put up barriers to protect ourselves. Imagine then that we go into a new relationship with an invisible fence around us. Some people's fences might be small, and over time they can unknowingly dismantle them, but others are like fortified fortresses and there's no getting in, however much your partner might try. That's what you are here for today – to try and identify why you've created your fence and to learn how to take it down. When you're surrounding yourself with a barrier you can never get close to anyone, and therefore never experience the intimacy that you're fundamentally craving for. Intimacy opens the door to compassion, and a relationship without compassion is a meaningless one. The truth is no one can do it for you, you are in control and must realize so if you want your life to change."

As he spoke I warmed to his no-nonsense approach. It made sense to me but also made me realize how many issues I had. He did some clever exercises to force us to be honest with ourselves – the kind that you didn't want to answer truthfully but felt you would be wasting your money if you didn't.

When he was in the flow of the final part of his lecture, a lady with a very loud voice stood up and interrupted him.

"This is all very well," she said, "but it's not what I came here for. You claimed to be able to offer a new approach to a loving relationship."

"That is what I am doing," he replied, not phased at all. "My approach is one of inner exploration to get the outer results that you are looking for. If something hasn't worked for you until now there's a clue that you need to change what you are doing, and I am offering a way to help you change. To make life better."

"This is waffle and I want my money back," she said angrily, as she picked up her bag and made her way towards the door. The room fell silent as virtually everyone watched her leave.

Our host waited patiently until she had closed the door behind her and faced the audience: "If you feel this isn't right for you, please feel free to leave. I don't offer a money back guarantee but I know what I teach is truth. It is wisdom handed down from many generations, and it is timeless in its simplicity. It applies to life itself – not just relationships."

Nobody moved and he finished his lecture.

As I walked away I knew I had gained a lot, and had finally accepted that I had to deal with the pain from my past and release its hold over me – then perhaps I would be able to open myself to intimacy instead of fearing it.

# CHAPTER TWENTY-SIX

It was a cold morning that greeted me as I opened the front door. I'd left it too late to book a taxi and got in the car hoping to find a parking space at the station. As usual I was in a rush, but not to get to the office – I was on my way to the London Television Studios to watch a series that was being filmed with Oprah. The show was based around a subject we wanted to cover in the magazine, and I was excited to hear the show. I made it just in time to hear her introduce her guests as I fumbled about getting my Dictaphone in working order. I looked up just as she was introducing her third guest and couldn't believe who was sitting on her sofa. I heard the words: "...to watch out for, whose unconventional views could take Britain by storm" and sat staring in disbelief. It wasn't what she said that shocked me, it was who she was talking about. Sitting on Oprah's sofa, right in front of me, was Mark Liscombe, my first love and the person I had come to realize I had never really gotten over. After reminiscing about our time together I had secretly prayed that he would come back into my life, but never believed it would actually happen. He looked more handsome than when we were younger, and I sat staring, trying to take in that Mark was actually sitting in front of me. I wanted to run up to him, but felt apprehensive as I wondered how he would greet me.

The show seemed to go on for hours as I sat waiting for it to finish, but as it came to a close it seemed too good to be true that I was minutes away from meeting Mark again. I had to remind myself that he was probably married and might have completely changed from the man I remembered him to be. A part of me was scared that I had built him up into something that he wasn't, and I tried to brace myself for what could be a disappointing reunion.

As soon as the filming had finished – and against the wishes of the floor manager – I made my way straight over to Mark. As

I got closer to him I caught his eye, and he stared at me for a moment as if he was trying to register how he knew me. Then he suddenly stood up and his face broke into the smile that I had always loved about him. He was beaming with a look of complete surprise.

"Oh my God, Alice, it's you. Oh my God, give me a hug. It's so good to see you, you look fantastic."

It was great to be hugged by him. He had filled out since the last time we had embraced one another and it felt so natural to be back in his arms.

"I can't believe it's really you, Alice. What the hell are you doing here? It's been so long?"

"I can't believe you were on the show. I just can't believe it. I don't know what to say. It's so good to see you."

"I've got a car coming in half an hour. How about we go upstairs and have a drink?"

I followed him through the back corridors of the studios until we reached the Green Room where drinks were being served. As we walked along I felt like we should have been holding hands. It had been so long since we'd seen each other but the spark was definitely still there. It was if there was an invisible cord that was pulling me closer to him – an excitement rising within me that I'd never experienced before. It had been over fifteen years since we had last seen each other and I had an overwhelming want to know everything about him, and what he had been doing in all the time we had lost contact.

It wasn't the right environment for us to catch up and I stood back for a while watching as he was approached by someone who started to ask him lots of questions. He had always been quite a confident person but he was different now – self-assured in an understated way. He finished his conversation quite abruptly and then surprised me by asking if I wanted to go somewhere else. We made our way to the taxi that was waiting for him. He suggested a restaurant, and within a few minutes we were there.

I wasn't really sure where to start when we finally sat down alone together, staring at an amazing view of the River Thames, with a soft white candle illuminating the middle of our table. He really was so much more handsome than I had remembered him to be and appeared so much more comfortable in himself – the boy who I had known all those years ago was now a man. I still couldn't comprehend that we had found each other.

We both had so much to say yet stayed silent for a while. It was as if we were inwardly acknowledging how much we had missed one another, with neither of us wanting to admit it. Eventually Mark broke the ice.

"It's been too long, Alice. You meant too much to me to have lived for so long without you in my life. It was so tough trying to get over you. I have never stopped thinking about you. This is the most perfect synchronicity that I have ever experienced."

I was stunned by how forthright he was. Yes, I had assumed that he had missed my friendship, but I hadn't expected him to still think about me. My stomach moved as if it was dancing to a fast-tempo feeling like I had just eaten a meal that I couldn't digest.

I felt too self-conscious to tell him that I had been thinking about him too, and sat uncomfortably thinking of what to say. He didn't seem to need a response from me and carried on regardless of my silence.

"I never stopped loving you, Alice. When I got my first publishing deal, all I could think about was wishing you were by my side to share in my happiness. It took four years of pushing before I got taken seriously and through all the trials all I could think about was you."

I couldn't believe what I was hearing; was he actually proclaiming his love for me – it was something I had only dreamed about and I wasn't ready to reply. Feeling embarrassed by what he was saying I changed the subject.

"I can't believe I haven't heard of your book or seen you being interviewed before."

"It's still quite niche even though we've sold over two million copies. It took a lot of courage to write what I did but I knew it was meant to be successful. I'm noticing more and more people getting deals based on similar subjects."

"Will you give me a copy of the book? I really want to read it, I'm intrigued."

"You'll be surprised by some of what I've written. It's really controversial. I've been condemned by some of the big corporates, and criticized by the medical industry and even some religious groups, but I don't care. I know what I've written is truth and so do the people who are backing me."

"You're not going to believe this but only a few months ago I was reminiscing about our conversations to do with religion and how you used to try and get me to be more open minded. I can't believe we're here now talking together. I want to pinch myself, it doesn't seem real. How the hell did you get into writing the book in the first place?"

"The day I admitted to myself that I was having a mental breakdown and screamed out loud: 'What's the meaning of my goddam pitiful life?' I was screaming like a madman at the top of my voice things like: 'I can't carry on any more; I can't cope. I hate my life. What the fuck is my life about other than to endure one nightmare after another?' You know I've always believed in a higher power and in that moment I was pleading to someone or something to give me some answers. When I finally fell asleep that night I had a dream that I remembered every detail of the next morning. I was walking through a dark tunnel with illuminated billboards on either side, there was something different written on each one and I just knew the words were directed at me. Each one summed up different things that had happened to me in the past, but from a strange perspective."

"What do you mean? What did they say?"

"I can still remember them so clearly. The detail comes

straight into my mind when I think about it. On one was written: 'You could only find your light by facing your darkness', another said: 'You chose your childhood to experience the pain of abandonment'. Another read: 'There is a reason behind every single thing that has happened to you'. Sorry, I bet this sounds ridiculous to you, doesn't it? Shall I shut up?"

"No, carry on. I'm fascinated."

"I know it sounds strange, but as I read each one I knew deep within me it was truth. I woke up knowing without doubt I was part of a bigger picture and that I was being protected. The true madness came when I tried to rationalize what it was I thought I was a part of, and who I thought was protecting me. Similar dreams happened for the following two weeks and I would wake up in the mornings and write down everything that I'd witnessed whilst I was supposed to be asleep. I began to see a pattern emerging – painful things that had happened to me in my past were being explained from a different perspective. I know that sounds weird but it's true. Then I started to get premonitions. I would see something in a dream, as if I was watching a film and then I'd turn on the news a few days later and watch the exact event actually happen. It didn't feel familiar as I watched it unfold, it felt freaky – something I couldn't explain to anyone. Oh God, I haven't stopped. Sorry."

"Carry on, this isn't as alien to me as you might think. I can't believe this has happened to you. I feel like I want to go into interviewer mode and ask you a hundred questions. How did you cope with what you were experiencing?"

"I knew I couldn't say anything to anyone, and started to go to bed really early wondering each night what would occur. I know it sounds crazy but although at first I thought I was dreaming I started to realize I was actually awake, and that's when the real questions started."

"What do you mean?"

"It was as if I was asking myself questions whilst I was asleep.

I know that doesn't make any sense."

"I'm trying to understand?"

"Ok, I'll give you an example. Bear with me. It was as if I was subconsciously asking myself questions, like: 'What is electricity? Explain electricity?' And the answer I got: 'You can't explain electricity. If you can you'll have an answer no scientist has yet come up with.' I'd never thought about electricity before, it was just something I took for granted, I guess like everyone does but then it got me thinking. I went straight onto the internet the next day to try and find an answer. Four hours later I was no wiser, other than I had a better understanding of protons and electrons, but there really was a mysterious element to it that I had never really considered before – something outside of rational explanation. Questions like that went on for about a week and turned into thinks like: 'Is history truth?' They were so profound that they rocked all the beliefs I had ever held before, making me question everything I had accepted as truth. By the end I felt fried, and that's when the real breakthrough happened."

"And what was that?"

"I realized there was a purpose to my life. Everything wasn't meaningless, but had happened for a reason. My faith in the force that was communicating with me got stronger and I started to believe all that I was being told."

"Bloody hell, so that's how the book came about?"

"Yep, that's basically how it all started, and believe me it's been a mad adventure ever since."

We were so engrossed in our conversation that neither of us had realized we were the last two people in the restaurant.

"They're ready to close," I said. "I think we should go. I so want to carry on talking but I need to get back. My mum's looking after my kids and doesn't like getting home late. She's so brilliant but I said I'd be home earlier. I had no idea we'd be talking like this. Oh God, I can't believe I haven't even mentioned that I've got children. We've got so much to catch up on."

# CHAPTER TWENTY-SIX

"Oh my God, how many children have you got?"

"Just the two – two boys but it often feels like more!"

"Are you married?" His tone felt cold – his openness suddenly contracted. "I can't believe what I've said to you. Sorry, Alice, I just assumed..." I followed his eyes as they fell on my wedding finger and interrupted him.

"Nope the ring-less finger says it all."

"Thank God – Christ, I thought I'd read my instincts wrongly. There's so much for us to talk about. I've got a bugger of a day tomorrow, are you free tomorrow night? Sorry...that sounded really presumptuous, I just want to spend more time talking to you, Alice. It's like a dream come true – you and me finding each other again. Imagine the odds – there's no way this is a coincidence."

There was such an amazing vulnerability about him, but also an invincible confidence. It was clear that he genuinely believed that life had brought us back together again. His assertiveness allowed me to be more forthcoming than I thought I'd be.

"I'd love to see you tomorrow." It felt so good to be open and honest. "Can we meet up after work?"

"I'm so sorry, Alice, I haven't asked anything about you. I haven't stopped talking. I'm so sorry. Where do you work?"

"At Isis magazine. Guess you've heard of it? Don't expect you to have read it."

"I lived with someone who loved that magazine – our toilet was piled high with them. I've been known to have a quick flick through," he said with a tweak in his eye and a playfulness he'd kept hidden.

As I left Mark that evening I felt amazing. The thrill of being back in his company was better than anything I could have ever imagined. It was like falling in love for the first time. I felt giddy with excitement about seeing him again and overwhelmed that we had come into contact in the most unsuspecting of circumstances. Did our dreams really come true when we least expected them to? Was there really truth in letting go of expectation to allow for the experience to happen of its own accord? I believed there was.

# CHAPTER TWENTY-SEVEN

I quickly discovered that Mark was divorced and not in a relationship, and so whilst we were both busy during the day, we made time to see each other in the evenings. Once the kids were in bed I just wanted to be with him – ideally every evening. We had so much to talk about and I was fascinated by what he had to say. The more he talked about his personal, illogical experiences the more intrigued I became about wanting to experience them for myself. I wanted to believe everything that he spoke about. To a cynic he sounded like a madman, but not to me. There were too many people writing about similar experiences to simply brush off what he was saying as insanity.

Over the next few months the depth of our friendship intensified and although he never mentioned again his love for me, he didn't hide the affection that he felt. I deliberately held back in telling him my feelings too. A part of me wanted to stay single just to avoid the pain of being hurt again, but I knew it would be different with him.

It didn't take long before Mark's friendship wasn't enough for me. I was finding him more attractive by the day. I felt like I would have to initiate something between us but there was still a part of me that was frightened of what could happen if I did.

A few weeks later Mark was invited to speak at the UN's headquarters in New York. After appearing on Oprah his career had sky rocketed. His unorthodox views seemed to have a place in more and more people's hearts and the demand for him to speak became unbelievable to both of us. He was elated that he'd been asked to speak alongside key figures in the peace movement and asked if I'd join him on the trip. I knew my mum would be happy to have the children, I was owed holiday from work and couldn't say yes quick enough.

We flew together to New York – and booked into separate rooms. Being away with one another made my feelings even stronger and it felt wrong that we weren't a couple. As I got ready for our first evening away, I got carried away thinking about Mark, daydreaming about kissing him, wishing we were sharing a room. A knock on my door interrupted my thoughts. I opened it slowly and stared at the most handsome man in the world. Mark looked fantastic: "My my, you scrub up well, Mr. Liscombe," I said as I looked up him, wishing he would kiss me.

"You look beautiful," he said staring directly into my eyes. I looped my arm around his and we made our way to the taxi.

As I watched him speak at the UN, tears trickled down my face. I was so proud of what he had become, and the courage it had taken to write what he had. He was making waves and doing what he believed in and I wanted to be a part of his world. I wanted to understand and know for myself all that he talked about – it was so peaceful yet so profound.

We stayed and listened to everyone else speak and then, not wanting the night to be over, found a bar close by that was open late. It was really busy and we made our way to the corner of the room that seemed quieter. We stood chatting for a while and then Mark looked like he had lost something as I watched him bend down and search on the floor. He looked awkward and I wondered what he was doing. The next thing I knew he was on one knee and looking up at me with a shy smile on his face. As he took my hand I started to laugh, and tried to get him to stand up, assuming he was joking with me.

"Alice?" he said resisting me tugging on him.

"Yes?" I said sarcastically, still not realizing he was being serious.

"Will you marry me?"

"Ha ha, Mark. Get up," I said as I pulled on his arm.

"I mean it, Alice, you are too precious to me to go on the way we are. I want you to be my wife. Please say yes to me."

As I realized he was actually proposing to me, I flung my arms around his neck and bent down to kiss him. Just before I pressed my lips against his I said, "Yes." I sat down on him cupping my legs around his back and we kissed for what seemed like an hour. Neither of us could stop or pull away and still locked together he lifted me up and lowered us down onto a chair. I was straddled across him and completely oblivious to anyone else in the bar.

"I love you," I said as tears streamed down my cheeks. "I love you so much. I can't believe this is happening. How can this be happening?"

"Because we're meant to be together. I never stopped loving you and prayed and prayed you would come back into my life. I still can't believe you're here, and now I'm never going to let you go. Please come with me to the Himalayas next week – I've taken the liberty of clearing it with your boss and your mum."

I was in shock.

In the back of the taxi on our way to the hotel Mark whispered into my ear, "I want to make love to you the minute we get back."

He said it in such an erotic way that I couldn't wait to get out of the taxi. The fear I thought I would encounter in thinking about having sex with him seemed to just disappear. It felt so natural to be together as we kissed in the lift and then walked hand in hand to my room. As I opened the door I grabbed Mark's hand and pulled him towards the bed. We stood staring at each other, and then I playfully pushed him backwards so that he fell onto the bed. I climbed on top of him and it felt amazing to feel him underneath me. As we kissed, he moved me so that we were lying on our sides facing one another. He gently removed my clothes piece by piece, leaving me naked, apart from my knickers. I reciprocated and then we pressed our bodies against one another, as he started to touch me in a way no one had ever done before. He stroked slowly along my shoulders and then down my back and then moved his hand to touch the front of me. I was in heaven, and as he ventured downwards he was met by the moist embrace of an area waiting for more than the feel of his fingers.

"I want you inside me," I whispered as the urge to make love became too strong to resist.

"I want to too but I don't want to rush you."

"You're not rushing me. Please, I'm ready."

I lay back and felt an unfamiliar sense of pleasure as he entered into me. I watched as he moved slowly within me, cautiously assessing my body language to ensure I wasn't feeling uncomfortable. I kissed his face and neck and then lifted my hips to beckon him to go deeper into me. He rolled us over so that I was on top of him and feeling completely uninhibited. I took his hands, and one at a time placed them on my breasts. He gently caressed my nipples as I lowered myself to take the whole of him within me. Slow movements led to a faster pace as I moved up and down, drawing him in deeper every time. As he started to move with me it was literally a matter of minutes before my body gave way and a pulse surged from the center of my being up to my head. The uncontrollable sudden jerks intensified and I was engulfed in a moment of pure peace and happiness.

The prude of the past had finally been laid to rest, and the seductress was firmly in her place. Passion was her path and intimacy her goal.

# CHAPTER TWENTY-EIGHT

Suddenly I was woken. He looked like a little goat herder with his walking stick and huge turban and for a moment I forgot where I was. The beauty of the Himalayas took my breath away and so did my wake up call. The etiquette of knocking before walking in had passed this young boy by as he stood staring at me, far too close to my bed for comfort.

"Madam, you must wake. You must wake."

"What's the time?" I asked sleepily.

He stared at me, not understanding what I was saying. I motioned to my wrist as if I was looking at the time and he hobbled out without saying anything. I assumed he'd be back, but he never returned.

I learnt at breakfast it was the only English phrase he knew, that had been perfected for the job of waking people up. He apparently had many tasks to attend to when he wasn't at school but this was the one he took most seriously. I mentioned to his parents, who owned the guest house, that a knock on the door would be perfectly sufficient but they just laughed, as if to say 'it's just his way, please get over it!' They were such humble, lovely people that I decided not to push the issue.

I rushed breakfast. I couldn't wait to see Mark after being apart for what felt like ages. The plan had been to spend ten days together in India but at the last minute he had been asked to fly to the Middle East as part of a UN peace initiative. Rather than cancel the holiday I had flown out ahead of him and now he was flying in to join me.

As I waited for the taxi to arrive to take me to the airport I was so excited about seeing Mark. From there we were heading high into the Himalayas to spend the week on a yoga retreat up in the mountains.

As I arrived at the airport I spotted Mark before he saw me

and ran up behind him and threw my arms around his waist. He turned around and I melted into the embrace that he gave me.

As the taxi climbed high into the hills we were both speechless as we stared out of the window, in awe at the beauty that surrounded us. There was something so magical about those mountains and the higher we went the more amazing it seemed to become.

As we arrived at our retreat we were greeted by a tiny, yet extremely toned man. In broken English he started to speak to us: "Air very special, you must try. Make you think different." We smiled and motioned as if to take a deep breath.

"You see," he said with a twinkle in his eye. "We and the mountain greet you. Mountain has power to transform, she very good to people. You be happy here."

Mark had warned me how differently yoga was practiced in the East, but I had had no idea just how watered down our version was.

It didn't take long before we both felt completely relaxed, as everyday opened my eyes to new possibilities I had never thought about before. I felt myself start to change in subtle ways. I had more energy and as I learnt to quiet my mind and focus in meditation my perceptions started to shift. It was as if outer layers of my consciousness were being imbued with new ways of thinking, allowing me to move closer to the inner part of my being that I had ignored for so long, having been oblivious to its existence.

Insight after insight led me to question the meaning of my life, and I suddenly realized how many of my previous experiences had been governed by the way I thought about them. I had often read in self-help books about the benefits of positive thinking, but had never been able to practically apply the theory. It was all very well being told to have positive thoughts about everything, but basically impossible when you hated your life and viewed it as anything but blissful. But new perspectives led me to new understandings and I no longer felt like the victim of my past experiences but the one in control of them.

Mark had the biggest transformation from our week away. He was approached by a yogi who was 108, but looked more like he was 70. He had an otherworldly aura about him and eyes that shone with wisdom. In a slightly disconcerting way he sat and stared at Mark one evening whilst we were having dinner, and then came over to our table and asked Mark why he wasn't using his healing skills.

"I heal people by getting them to connect with the true essence of themselves," Mark said in a slightly suspicious way. But the yogi wasn't satisfied.

"Your hands are blessed with divine gifts," he said as he held Mark's hands and turned them upwards.

"They are needed in the West more than any medicines. Man is making himself worse by the very acts that he thinks are making him better. You must believe in your gifts and use them wisely. People desperately need the miracles that can flow through you if you allow them to. You must believe or they will not reveal themselves to you."

No longer suspicious, Mark was intrigued by what the yogi had to say. Something in him knew it was true and he spent the rest of the week trying to nurture the gifts that were to change our lives forever.

I left India a completely different person. My inner strength had deepened and I vowed I wanted to return to the UK and do something more meaningful with my life. Being in those mountains was so inspiring and it made me appreciate how powerful individuals could be. I'd thought a lot about the yoga movement in the West, and how one man from the East had been initially responsible for introducing the concept, revolutionizing the way so many people exercised. Millions were now reaping the benefits of an exercise that focused on uniting mind, body and spirit – allowing you to relax and rejuvenate, being conscious of the present moment, whilst toning your body all at the same time. Whilst the East was aware of the many deeper reasons to enjoy yoga, we were slowly starting to acknowledge some of the more subtle benefits of using your mind and body to initiate a new understanding of yourself and the world around you – something that would have seemed ludicrous not so long ago.

When I returned to work I felt like I'd left a part of me in those mountains. Everything I looked at was from a new perspective and I started to believe and feel that there was purpose to my life. The East's view of turning inwards was having a huge impact on me, as my inner reality became more real by the day.

I had a meeting with my editor and asked if I could write an article about spirituality in the East and its growing influence on the West. Technically it wasn't a subject that affected our readers but I was determined to make it one, and help women understand its benefits at a practical level.

"I don't see why not," she said, surprising me. I had expected an outright 'no' and felt excited by her seeming enthusiasm. "But I want you to be really careful about the angle that you take. It can't be preachy and it's got to be relevant – if you manage to do that then I'll let you run with the feature."

I already had an idea for the article which I put to her over lunch.

"That's too controversial," she said straight away. "I was thinking more along the lines of applying some of the philosophy to women's domestic issues."

"I understand what you're saying," I said, really wishing I could tackle some heavier issues.

"Do you know what, Alice? We're getting into dodgy territory. Do me a favor and just stick with sex and relationships. It's working so well and our figures are up on all the other glossies.

People have too many worries close to home to be thinking about this sort of stuff. I don't want to start changing our editorial stance now, especially not in this economic climate. I think it's best we avoid it altogether. Sorry."

She had a point and I decided to drop the idea. But the need for me to do something related to what I had learnt in those mountains was too strong for me to ignore.

# CHAPTER TWENTY-NINE

It took another six months before I realized that the combination of Mark and my strengths was a winning formula. He had the deep belief in a new vision for the world – and the gifts to help it happen – and I had the passion to want to do something to help alleviate people's suffering. We sat up night after night working out how we could combine our skills, and do our part in making a small difference to a world being slowly brought to its knees.

It didn't take long to see our first step. There was a huge void opening up that was easy to ignore yet was staring us in the face. The country was sliding into a depression and as a result people's emotional states were reflecting the economic situation. It was as if we were at a cultural stalemate as people mourned the loss of the jobs and possessions that they had come to claim as representing who they were. The foundations of our culture were literally being rocked as the very things people had striven so hard to achieve were being stripped away from them. As the media spun more and more doom and gloom, even people who were financially comfortable were starting to be affected by the negativity that was emanating from everywhere.

We knew we needed to use Mark's skills as a healer on a bigger scale. He was spending his time travelling to wherever there was demand for him, but the belief in what he could do was building momentum. Despite all the skeptics, he had been dubbed the 'Miracle Man', and attention was growing as to how he was actually able to cure people so quickly and without any medicine.

Our plan was to start a healing center that would help to alleviate people's physical and emotional problems – focusing mainly on the inner world of the person. We wanted the center to be somewhere that people could stay for a few weeks, or visit as a one off. Overall, the atmosphere would be invigorating and relaxing with the hope that people left feeling transformed ideally both physically and mentally. We were aware that it would mostly draw the wealthy to start off with, but our goal was to gain huge funding to cater for those in financial turmoil too.

Over the next month we completed a business plan for our 'Centre for Inner Peace' and started to think about funding. Whilst it was the worst time to be starting a new business we knew it would be a success and instinctively knew we had to convince like-minded people to back our idea. We enlisted the help of two of our good friends, Paul and Amber, who had enthused about the center from the moment we had spoken about it. Being well-known alternative therapists themselves they wanted to help us build on our idea, and then work for the center when we finally opened.

Once Mark and I made our decision to commit one hundred per cent to the plan, we both seemed to gain an energy that allowed us to get by on little sleep, yet function far more creatively than either of us had ever done before.

The long hours paid off and it wasn't long before we had the funding, the location and a few celebrity backers to champion our cause. The editor of Isis was a great help and put us in touch with her husband who was a property developer. We assumed he would help us to find a location, but after a formal meeting that was more business-like than either of us had expected, he mentioned that he was considering giving us some land. We were amazed by how much they had both bought into our vision and left the meeting excited by what he would come back and offer us.

The following day he called and asked us to drive with him to Essex, to view a twenty-five acre plot of land that he had been forced to leave derelict due to the government's ban on residential new-builds. He believed it would be over ten years before he would legally be able to build houses on the site, and agreed to give us the land in return for us rewarding him with the building contract. A number of huge old barns stood on the land and we immediately agreed that they could be used for the center.

We worried slightly about the location and accessibility to the rest of the country, but whilst it may not have seemed ideal at first, we were to learn that people would travel from across the country – and then the world – to visit our sanctuary.

It took a huge amount of work but a year from the day we were donated the land, we were ready to open our doors to the public. We decided to make the opening a grand affair – determined not to be labeled as new-age hippies – and with the help of a few known faces we generated a lot of publicity for ourselves. Before we knew it the first three hundred people had walked through our doors. Word of mouth proved to be a very powerful tool, and without the need for any paid marketing within three months we had welcomed over two thousand people. Mark, Paul and Amber obviously couldn't cope with the demand alone and very quickly more people joined us, alongside the staff that enabled the center to run efficiently.

It wasn't long before we offered weekend retreats – which were a combination of alternative therapies, meditation and physical healing – but the environment wasn't squeaky clean. Being a smoker myself it felt wrong to make people feel uncomfortable about a habit that was so hard to quit, and so we did what no other holistic environment had ever considered doing. To the astonishment and criticism of many we created a relaxing indoor smoking area, equipped with state-of-the-art air suction units, and devices that blew in aromatherapy oils to counteract the smell of the smoke. Next to the smoking room was a bar that was always stocked to the brim. We wanted to avoid people feeling intimated by the environment and found the bar area to be the heart of the center. There was such a buzz around the place at night, especially when we invited guest musicians to perform. It was a quirky environment and looking back I suppose it was inevitable that we would attract celebrities and huge amounts of press coverage – but we never expected it to spiral like it did. Some of the most popular times of the year were when we invited guest speakers to come a share some of themselves with an audience that often numbered over a thousand people.

The center grew so quickly, and within another year we had to extend our guest bedroom area and add additional treatment rooms. We kept all the buildings in the style of converted barns, with the main center enjoying contemporary designs with floor to ceiling windows and huge skylights. Candles and aromatherapy oils burned everywhere, helping people to feel relaxed from the moment they walked through our doors. The meditation room offered a direct view of the sky with its glass dome ceiling and seats that were so comfortable that people would often fall asleep in them.

What we hadn't bargained for was how much Mark's healing skills would be in demand, with people coming from across the world to be cured by him. His work was becoming so controversial that many respected doctors were speaking out against him – yet for all the negative press doubting his abilities there were the stories of those who had been cured, who swore by what he could do. The debate was wide open and the medical industry was trying hard to shut us down and discredit what we were doing. Drug-free rehabilitation wasn't on their agenda and they did everything they could to make sure we weren't taken seriously. But they had misjudged the human spirit's inherent quest to find the truth and the more they tried to undermine us, the more they pushed people to visit our center and come to their own conclusions.

# CHAPTER THIRTY

Whilst Mark, Paul and Amber were the real story behind our center, by default I became the spokesperson, and therefore the one the public associated with everything we did. Yet it wasn't long before the press had other ideas for me. One minute I was busy building and expanding something I believed passionately about, and the next I had been catapulted into the limelight and given celebrity status. I was labeled the 'Peace Guru' and suddenly there were pictures of me everywhere. The image created from day one was that I spent my time hanging out with celebrities and there was nothing I could do to stop the fervor that was literally whisked-up overnight.

The celebrity link had come about as a result of people visiting the center. It was such an informal environment that we often ended up talking late into the night, and it became natural that as a result of the friendships we forged, people offered to use their fame to help us. After they left it was usually within days that we received an invitation either to visit them at their homes or meet in London. Of course we made the effort to go. Bonds had been built and their offers of wanting to be involved were genuine – and of course being in their company normally guaranteed a fun night out. Mark and I always went out together, but with him having been the cause of so much controversy, the press decided that I was the better story. It was as if they had colluded overnight to create a celebrity out of me and the result was that they started to follow us everywhere we went.

I often wondered during that time how it was for famous celebrities who were suddenly pushed into the limelight. There was something so uncomfortable about being made into a brand that others were encouraged to idolize.

I had virtually forgotten about Sam at that point in my life until I realized that it was only a matter of time before he would see my face splashed across the British press. I wondered if he had really given up on getting back at me, and knew my newfound publicity would rile him.

I should have known that he would use the opportunity to try and discredit me, and it wasn't long before he emerged on a mission to supposedly tell Britain the truth about me. In an exclusive interview he allegedly revealed how heartless I really was, and how awful I had been to him. Whilst no one else would publish his revelations, this particular paper ran further interviews that led to Sam being invited by a well-known talk-show host. As much as I didn't want to read or listen to what he said, my curiosity got the better of me and I couldn't believe the lies he spun about me.

I was advised to sue him for defamation but knew it was a pointless exercise that would only give him further exposure. Instead, I decided to ignore him in the hope that he would exhaust what he had to say and would no longer be of interest to the media.

I still have no idea how they initially got together, but soon after Sam's appearances in the press he started dating actress and singer Sonia Burns. Having exhausted his options trying to defame me, he gained publicity playing the part of victimized husband turned victor as he gushed about how happy he was with Sonia. I worried as I looked at pictures of the two of them together – she seemed smitten and I hoped her fate wouldn't lie where mine had done with Sam. I gathered that she was stronger than me and in a much better position, but a part of me was concerned for her, despite her high public profile and huge wealth.

Sam had claimed in an interview that he could no longer see his sons because of the abuse he would have to endure if he came near me. There was obviously the begging question that they could go to him if Sam was so worried about me attacking him, but the reporter had failed to cross-question him as to how ludicrous his excuse was. I wondered if Sonia believed the reason that Sam had given, in that he didn't see his children because of me.

A mutual friend of mine and Sonia's wanted to make her aware that I had not stopped Sam from seeing his children, but rather than push the issue I decided to let it lie, at least for a while. I knew he really had chosen to cut off from them and in a selfish way I was relieved that there was no contact, aware that he would only try and turn them against me if he saw them. Luckily Sam's fame was short-lived and after a flurry in the media he was no longer an interesting story to them. Every so often he was pictured at various parties and award ceremonies with Sonia but that was all. It was as if the media would no longer let him use them to try and get back at me.

# CHAPTER THIRTY-ONE

Sam's attempts to discredit me had the reverse effect and I came to benefit from his attacks on me. More and more journalists wanted to know what our center was all about, and the result was that we were receiving one positive review after the other.

Whilst all the publicity did wonders for the center, our real turning point came when a famous actor visited us, after suffering from a very public humiliating break-up. He had a deep understanding of mind, body and spirit and wanted to spend two weeks at the center to try and get to the bottom of much of the pain from his life. Although known to the world by day as a famous actor, when time permitted he chameleoned into a humanitarian, set on wanting to make a difference to the world. As we got to know him he told us how he had spent months devising a plan to bring about change to a small part of the world, and was waiting for the right time to put the idea into action. It was a grand plan and one that he needed many people for, but when he approached us a few months later and asked for our help, what he suggested was on a scale that seemed unfathomable at first.

He had watched intensely as Darfur slid into an atrocity that most people were oblivious to. Yes, it was on the news bulletins all the time, but with everyone struggling to cope under the pressure of the depression it was ignored – yet to him the news of the genocide spoke directly to his heart. Whilst for many Darfur was a remote part of the world, populated with peoples that they couldn't relate to, for Aaron it felt like the atrocities were happening to his friends. Not being a religious man, he blushed as he explained it felt like his calling to help the situation as Darfur had particular significance to him. Eight years previously he had spent three months on location in

Khartoum, Sudan. After befriending his local driver, he was invited to visit the man's family home. The man lived in the western province of Darfur, and for three days Aaron and two of his colleagues enjoyed what he described as unrivalled hospitality. Whilst they were there they met many locals and came to respect their deep family values and reverence for their surroundings. Their self-sufficiency and love for one another left their mark on him as he returned to the big city and carried on his life as a world-renowned actor.

The more he understood about the truth of what was happening in the region, the more determined he became to personally do something about it. His plan initially involved helping the victims of the conflict, predominately the women and children. The area was too dangerous for an overt operation, so using his contacts inside Darfur he had devised a way to secretly get in and out – a plan that would put most military strategists to shame. His intention was to remove the women and children that wanted to go and get them to safety and to an environment that was way beyond anything a refugee camp could offer them. Although he wanted to provide the men protection to evacuate too, he had been warned that the men would stay and defend their villages to the bitter end. Once the women and children were brought to safety he wanted to send in a private military force to work alongside the men to defeat the barbarians who were pillaging their villages. He had been helped with his plan by a friend who was ex-MI6 who had led him to endless contacts in the intelligence field. It was a grand plan that had been thought about meticulously with every detail covered.

Aaron pleaded with Mark and I to be involved in what at first seemed like an overambitious idea. He wanted us to set up a center for the women and children to go to once they had been evacuated – a sort of extension of our own center. It sounded like a huge task at first but the more we thought about it the more it seemed like a natural progression for us to broaden out to parts of the world that were most crying out for help.

Once Mark and I committed to becoming part of Aaron's plan, we set about trying to fundraise to build the center. With his help and contacts, our collective ability to raise money was mind blowing. It was as if the world was in such a state that those who had money genuinely wanted to do whatever they could to ease their guilt.

With so much help behind us, our African center became a reality very quickly, and it wasn't long before we were able to give Aaron the go ahead to execute his plan.

Whilst we took care of all the women and children, trying to help them rehabilitate with a program that aimed to heal them physically and emotionally, the military arm of the operation ended up expanding to the point where they overthrew the Sudanese government, installing by proxy a genuinely good man to run the country. He wasn't left alone however, and to this day a very close eye is kept upon him and the area as a whole.

We all agreed to also take on the rebuilding of the area so that Darfur's people could return to their homeland and live in dignity. Taking into consideration the drought suffered by the region we used an Israeli form of irrigation and water distribution, alongside other systems to ensure the area would be self-sufficient and no longer left to perish in poverty and famine.

Again by default I became the spokesperson for the operation, and the more I spoke the more I realized what an amazing feat we had all achieved. By the end of 'Operation Freedom', and with so many powerful people onboard, it became obvious how effective we could be. Before Darfur was properly restored we were onto planning our next mission. We wanted to look closer to home knowing that the time was right to start asserting the need for change – we wouldn't just speak about it, we would take the action to bring it about as well.

I'm not sure to this day if it was the press, the celebrity contacts, or the genuine desire to make a difference that catapulted my life into a direction I could never have imagined. It was as if a force far bigger than all of us individually was willing us on, putting in front of us the tools, people and plans to help bring peace to a world that was on the brink of self-destruction.

Within a few years we were achieving peace in small pockets of the world and the ripple effects were astounding. We were helping Africa to start to stand up for herself through self-sufficiency and dismantling the corrupt regimes. Yes, we were being fought against – there were many trying to stop us, but our intelligence was too great, and manpower too strong. The collective voice at home was starting to demand change too and the powers that-be were being forced to give a shit. The PR spin that had worked for them in the past was no longer being accepted as the demand for truth became impossible for them to ignore. The more we pushed for change the more popular what we were trying to achieve became, and the more people came forward to help us – to the extent that was unbelievable to all of us. It was co-operation on a scale that philosophers of the past could have only dreamt about. People everywhere, using their power to bring about good – for themselves and those around them. Some with greater means, giving on scales that would be unfathomable at any other time in history.

There was still a huge way to go but the psyche was changing and the biggest threat to peace was now being threatened by its very own propaganda. War as a means to bringing about security, peace and hope started to seem so ludicrous to people that it was as if for all the years we had allowed it to be so, we had been in some kind of slumber. How had it been that for so long we had believed in violence as a solution to peace? Yet whilst the logic was staring everyone in the face, we couldn't do a damn thing about it, because the beast had become so much bigger than the people. But as history proves time and time again, and like the fate of the Roman Empire, tyrannical rule is always brought down. Perhaps not as quickly as we would hope, but when people are brought to their knees, becoming slaves to the very system that's promising their freedom, it's inevitable for change to occur.

I turned on the television just in time to hear the end of Aaron's televised speech. He was such a brilliant orator and delivered words to an audience that left most world leaders wishing they could emanate. He was speaking on behalf of the operation and as always his words were as profound as his actions.

"People are powerful. Let this be a warning to anyone trying to stop change. We are stepping into a new era. A time of co-operation, a time of compassion. A time when old values are falling away. A time when people are being called into action, and a time when those opposing change will be called into account."

I watched the camera fade away from him and felt proud of what we were achieving. It was only the start but times were definitely changing for the better.

I looked at Mark and kissed him. We had come such a long way from the days sat in my house trying to figure out what we could do together, but now we were both exhausted and couldn't wait for our holiday the following day. A time away from the eyes of the world where we could enjoy one and other amongst the beautiful backdrop of the Caribbean.

# EPILOGUE

They say through pain you grow. A cliché yes, but in my life it's been true. We all have a choice – to sink or swim when the going gets tough. Sometimes the most hurtful experiences can open the doors to our biggest breakthroughs. Our weakest moments can be the catalysts to showing us strengths we didn't even know we had. Some say it's crap, that it can't be true – that life's a bitch and then you die. But to believe there's no meaning to it all – where does that leave us? Does a soulless, shallow life really bring happiness? What's happened to living with passion and finding real pleasure in doing something we love to do? Then again, what does 'love' mean anyway? Where's its place now? Is it just some ancient ideal that will be written about in text books as something lost and forgotten? We've let so many things become extinct. Are we really ready to leave love behind? Isn't it the real cog that could make the world a better place? Isn't it our most basic, natural yearning to love and be loved back? Money might have become the driving force for most of us, but is money without love really a winning combination? Maybe it is for you? Love is one of the only things in the world that can't be bought, yet when it's given it can move us more than anything else could ever do.

# THIS IS YOUR LIFE.

DO WHAT YOU LOVE,
AND DO IT OFTEN.

IF YOU DON'T LIKE SOMETHING, CHANGE IT.

## IF YOU DON'T LIKE YOUR JOB, QUIT.

IF YOU DON'T HAVE ENOUGH TIME, STOP WATCHING TV.
IF YOU ARE LOOKING FOR THE LOVE OF YOUR LIFE, STOP;
THEY WILL BE WAITING FOR YOU WHEN YOU

## START DOING THINGS YOU LOVE.

STOP OVER ANALYZING, ALL EMOTIONS ARE BEAUTIFUL.

## LIFE IS SIMPLE. WHEN YOU EAT, APPRECIATE EVERY LAST BITE.

OPEN YOUR MIND, ARMS, AND HEART TO NEW THINGS
AND PEOPLE, WE ARE UNITED IN OUR DIFFERENCES.
ASK THE NEXT PERSON YOU SEE WHAT THEIR PASSION IS,
AND SHARE YOUR INSPIRING DREAM WITH THEM.

## TRAVEL OFTEN; GETTING LOST WILL HELP YOU FIND YOURSELF.

SOME OPPORTUNITIES ONLY COME ONCE, SEIZE THEM.
LIFE IS ABOUT THE PEOPLE YOU MEET, AND
THE THINGS YOU CREATE WITH THEM
SO GO OUT AND START CREATING.

## LIFE IS SHORT. LIVE YOUR DREAM AND SHARE YOUR PASSION.

"THE HOLSTEE MANIFESTO" ©2009    WRITTEN BY DAVE, MIKE & FABIAN    DESIGN BY RACHAEL    WWW.HOLSTEE.COM/MANIFESTO

At Roundfire we publish great stories. We lean towards the spiritual and thought-provoking. But whether it's literary or popular, a gentle tale or a pulsating thriller, the connecting theme in all Roundfire fiction titles is that once you pick them up you won't want to put them down.